T0355033

DAMAGED

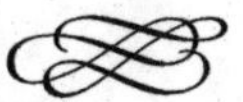

WILLOW WINTERS

ABOUT

I married the bad boy from Brooklyn.

The one with the tattoos and the look in his eyes that told me he was bad news.

The look that came with all sorts of warnings.

I knew what I was doing.

I knew by the way he put his hands on me, how he owned me with his forceful touch.

I couldn't say no to him, not that I wanted to.

That was then, and it seems like forever ago.

Years later, I've grown up and moved on. But he's still the man I married. Dangerous in ways I don't like to think about. Sexy as sin, he attracts all the wrong kinds of temptations.

The kind that's unforgivable.

The kind that splits up marriages.

I did this to myself. I knew better than to love him.

And now I'm fucked.

I married the bad boy from Brooklyn. And I don't know how I'll survive this.

PREFACE

Kat

It only took one night; one moment, and my fate was sealed. He knew I would never tell him no.

I wonder what would have happened if I'd never met Evan. The thought makes my stomach sink and twist, and a cold chill flows in waves over my body.

It *pains* me. It literally hurts to think about not having him in my life. I didn't know I was setting myself up for heartbreak all those years ago. Yet here I am, and that reality is what keeps me up at night.

That chance encounter set everything into motion, and I would have said it was a blessing only months ago. But now I know better.

PREFACE

I wish I'd never stopped.

I wish I'd never met Evan.

Whoever said it's better to have loved and lost than never to have loved at all was a liar and a fool.

This isn't worth it.

If only I could go back.

CHAPTER 1

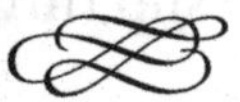

Kat

Tell me a lie and make it sweet,
Like the vows you made on our wedding day.
Tell me a lie, don't make it hurt,
The pain in my chest just won't go away.
Don't tell me the truth, I can't face what's to come.
I'll yell and I'll kick, I'll fight it, I'll run.
Don't tell me the truth, I don't want to hear.
Tell me pretty lies with whispers sincere.

My skin feels cold. It's an odd sensation that travels across my arms and I'd like to blame it on the alcohol, but I've felt it all day. Before the drinks came easier and easier. For *days,* really, I've been feeling this weird sense of not quite being my my own body. Maybe weeks, but I've been ignoring the signs and whispers, pretending like they weren't real.

But this sickness won't leave me, now that I can't deny it.

Ever since I let the words slip through my lips.

I hate you.

You're a fucking liar.

I want a divorce.

The tears prick my eyes, but I don't let them fall. Instead a shuddering breath leaves my lips and I lift my glass up, downing the remaining wine. It's too sweet for being so dark.

The glass nearly tips as I set it down quickly to wipe under my eyes. I don't want him to see me cry; I won't let him. But the creak at the top of the stairs was a false alarm. I don't hear the heavy sound of him coming down the steps to our townhouse. Instead I'm still alone on the first floor dining room, waiting for him to leave.

The thick, dark drapes behind me are pulled shut but even they can't completely drown out the night sounds of busy New York City outside. There's always a bit that travels through. It used to bother me when I moved here initially, but now it's soothing. It calms me as I look past the open room toward the empty stairwell.

I shouldn't be drunk, sitting at the head of the dining room table when I'm supposed to be preparing to meet with a potential client. I'm damn good at what I do, one of the top agents in New York City, but tonight, I don't care.

I shouldn't have closed my laptop and logged off of all social media when I have promotions and advertisements running around the clock for these launches.

I shouldn't be doing a lot of things.

But here I am, and I refuse to do anything but watch the stairs and wait for him to leave.

I listen carefully as I pour the last of the wine from the bottle into the glass. He's packing, like he always does, but this time it's so much different. He's traveling for work, but when he leaves from his rendezvous in London, he's not coming back here.

"He better not," I mutter beneath my breath at the thought.

I lift the glass back to my lips, the dark cabernet tasting sweeter and sweeter with each sip, lulling me into a languor where the memory of yesterday fades.

Where the article doesn't exist. Where the admission of an affair can fall on deaf ears. The picture itself was innocent. But Evan doesn't have a single explanation for me. He can't make clear to me why he's lying, why he's stuttering over his words to come up with a justification.

What hurts the most is the look in his eyes. It's his boss' wife, in the middle of a vicious divorce. And he was with her at 3 in the morning in her hotel lobby.

There's only one explanation for that. Even he can't come up with a reason, *although he still denies it*. It's a slap in my face. And I'm done pretending like I can forgive him for this.

I suck in a long, deep breath, pushing the phone away as it beeps again with a message from a friend and I lean back in my chair. I don't want to hear it. I cover my eyes with my hands, suddenly feeling hot. Too hot.

They keep asking me the same things, but with different words.

Are you alright? - Maddie

Is it true? - Julia

So you finally went through with it? – Suzette

Messages from each of my friends hit my phone one by

one, each of them making it vibrate on the table throughout the day.

It takes everything in me to face them, as if they were really here asking me all these questions in person. I don't have answers to give them, none that I want to say out loud anyway. I'm not pushing my husband away because I want to. I'm only doing it because I have to and I don't have the resolve to speak that confession. Even I'm disappointed in myself.

My friends want what's best for me. They want to help me and I know that's the truth, but it doesn't keep me from being angry at the phone as it goes off again.

Just leave me alone. Everyone get out of my life, *my marriage*. It wasn't for them to see. It's not for them to judge. Like every other fucking gossip column in New York City. It's not the first time our marriage was mentioned in the papers, but I pray it'll be the last.

My knuckles turn white as I grip the phone with the intent on throwing it, silencing it and letting it smack against the wall, but I don't. It's the sound of Evan's boots rhythmically hitting each step as he walks down the stairs that forces me to compose myself.

I stare at the small strip of red on the silence button as I flip the switch off on my phone and ignore the texts and calls, squaring my shoulders as I attempt to pull myself together.

I haven't answered a single one since this morning when Page Six came out with the article about our separation. It's funny how I only uttered the words two nights ago, yet it's already on social media, circulating gossip columns. I wonder if he wanted this. If that was Evan's way of finally pushing his workaholic wife to the brink of divorce.

My gaze morphs into a glare as he comes into view, but it doesn't stay long. My skin is suddenly feeling hotter, but in a way that's joined with desire. I can just imagine how his rough stubble would feel against my palm and how his lips would taste as he leans down to kiss me goodbye. It's funny how the goodbye kisses are the ones I value most, but I won't let him kiss me before he leaves this time.

Even if he is only wearing a pair of faded jeans and a plain white t-shirt, he's still devilishly handsome. It's his muscular physique and tanned, tattooed skin that let him get away with a classic bad boy look regardless of what he has on. My heart beats slower and slower as the seconds pass between us; it's calming just to look at him. That's how he got me in the beginning. The desire and attraction I feel are undeniable.

He's the first to break the gaze as he runs his fingers through his dark brown hair and lets out an uneasy sigh. And my lips curl into a sarcastic smile, mocking both me and my thoughts. I'm not the only one to fall for his charm and allure, but I should have already learned my lesson. My fingers slip down the thin stem of the wine-glass as I smile weakly and force the sting in my eyes to go away, pretending I'm not going to cry, pretending that I've made my decision final. Like I don't already regret it.

"I have to go," he says after a moment of uncomfortable silence.

My blood rushes and I try to swallow the lump in my throat. I focus on the wine, the dark red liquid pooling into the base of the glass. I try to swirl it, but it doesn't move, there's so little left.

"Is she going to be there?" I ask him, staring straight ahead at a black and white photo of the two of us taken years ago on vacation in Mexico. I look at my genuine smile and how he has his arm wrapped possessively around me as he answers. I hate that I even bothered to ask. It's my insecurity, my hate, my envy even.

"No, she's not. And I already told you it doesn't matter." Any trace of a smile or even of disinterest leaves me. I can't hide what it does to me, what his lie has done to me.

My elbow rests on the table as I sit my chin in my hand

and try to cover up how much it hurts. To keep it from him just like he's keeping the truth from me. I speak low and stare straight ahead. "You told me it's not true, but you didn't deny it to the press," I tell him and finally look him in the eyes. "You didn't deny it to anyone but me, and I know you're lying." My words crack at the end and I have to tear my eyes away.

Everyone told me and warned me five years ago when I first started seeing him. I knew what I was doing when I first said yes to him, when I gave myself to him and let myself fall for someone like him. I'm a fool.

"I told you, it's not what it looks like," he says softly, like he's afraid to say the words louder.

"Then why not tell them?" I ask him in a wounded voice. "Why let the world believe you've cheated on me? What could you possibly gain?" Each question gets louder as the words rush out of my mouth. I'm ashamed of how much passion there is in my voice. How much pain is on display.

I know why he doesn't deny it to them, and it's because it's true. Years of just the two of us have told me who he is and I know he's not a liar, but he's lying to me now. I've never been more sure of anything in my life. "It's been weeks, hasn't it?" I force the words out. Last night I couldn't talk without screaming. Without slamming my fists into the table, making it shake and breaking a glass of water that tipped and shattered on the hardwood floors.

I reached my breaking point when he looked me in the eye and told me there was nothing to that picture. I won't listen when he lies; not when he does such a horrific job of it.

"Stop it, Kat," Evan says firmly, and his voice is harsh and unforgiving, like I'm the one in the wrong.

"Oh I see," I tell him, raising a brow and feeling that sick smile tug at my lips. "You cheat, you lie, but I should be quiet and give you a kiss on the way out to go back to her?"

"Don't do this," he says with a rawness that makes my heart clench.

"Then tell me what happened. I know something did." For weeks he's been distant, cold toward me even.

A moment passes and I lose my composure again, bared to him in every way as I wait for an answer. But I don't get the one thing I need. The truth. *Or a believable lie.*

"I have to go," he says and slings the black duffle bag over his shoulder, gripping the suitcase with his other hand. "I love you."

He says the words without looking at me.

“If you don’t tell me the truth,” I speak lowly as I stare at the table, pushing each word out and feeling them slice open the cut in my heart that much deeper, “then don’t bother coming back.” My throat tightens and my lungs refuse to fill as silence is all that answers me.

He leaves without attempting to kiss me or coming close to me in the least. His strides don’t break in cadence until the heavy walnut front door opens and closes, leaving me with nothing but the tortured sob that’s desperate to come up and the faint sounds of the city life filling the empty space once again.

My hands tremble as I close my eyes and try to calm down.

If he really loved me, he wouldn’t have let it come to this.

If he loved me, he’d tell me the truth.

Secrets break up marriages.

I keep telling myself that he’s to blame, but as a cry rips up my throat and I bring my knees into my chest, the heels of my feet resting on the seat of the chair, I replay the last few years and I know I’m at fault. Deep down, I know. I bury my face in my knees and rock slightly, feeling pathetic as I break down yet again.

If I was him, I'd have cheated on me too.

He says he didn't. He swears it's a lie.

But he doesn't explain it. He can't even look me in the eye.

I did this to myself. I should've known better.

CHAPTER 2

Evan

Death comes to all but in different ways,
At times so beautiful, counting down the days.
Lies and deceit are a bit the same,
Some so familiar they flow in your veins.
Others play tricks and laugh so hard they shake,
While they cause you nothing but brutal heartache.
It's hard to outrun them, even harder to fool.
One thing can't be denied-
Sins and secrets are nothing but cruel.

When did I turn into the piece of shit I am right now?

Pathetic. That's how I feel as the plane rumbles beneath my feet and I shake my head slightly, waving off the flight attendant and whatever small bag of snacks she was offering me.

I crack my neck to the left and right as a ding indicates the seatbelt sign is off and everyone can move about the cabin. I have no intention of getting up or doing a damn thing but sit here and try to figure out exactly where it all went wrong.

The Wi-Fi is available and I take my time setting it up, prolonging the moment when I'll have to face the fact that she hasn't messaged me. She can yell at me, hit me, take it all out on me, but her silence last night is what kills me. Her shutting me out is something like a knife to the heart.

There's no way to make it right, but I'm not letting her go.

Kat's mine. My wife. *My love.*

And I couldn't even kiss her before leaving. She's kidding herself if she thinks I'm not coming home to her. I don't care that we're going through this, I don't care how bad our fight is or that I fucked up beyond repair. She doesn't know what happened and I hope she never will, but that doesn't change the fact that she's mine.

I clear my throat and clench my teeth as the plane

rumbles again, reminding me that she's miles and miles away. Reminding me that I left her again.

I can't bring myself to feel like I deserve her forgiveness. Like I deserve her at all. The guilt is all-consuming and now I'm trapped in a corner, desperately looking for a way out of the mess I've gotten myself into.

My computer pings as the plane continues to fly across the ocean taking me farther away from her, and I lean forward to check it. I'm quick to do it too, praying it's Kat.

Praying's never helped me before, and sure enough it didn't this time either. It's just James, my boss and Samantha's now ex.

My teeth grind against one another as I read the message. It's the schedule for the rest of the day and my room number for the hotel.

But it feels like a slap in the face. I can't keep this up and live each day as if nothing's happened. Pretending like nothing's changed.

My head pushes into the seat as I take a calming breath.

Stuck between a rock and a hard place is an inadequate saying.

I'm fucked. Just waiting for them to pick, pick, pick away at me while I have my hands tied behind my back.

Only years ago, I loved my life. This is what I wanted more than anything. On the outside, it's glamorous. I'll be staying at a five-star resort, partying with celebrities and having every sinful pleasure at my fingertips. That's what a life of avoiding prison has given me.

I protect the clients from any bad press, keep charges from sticking, and avoid any altercations that could lead to something … unwanted. And in return, I'm paid generously and live the high life.

I didn't sign up for *this* though, but I sure as fuck cashed every check along the way. My email beeps and it's another message from James, as if confirming this is exactly what I signed up for. It's what I asked for.

Let me know when you land. That's all the email says.

I clear my throat as my hand balls into a fist and I run the rough pad of my thumb over my knuckles slowly. I can see my reflection in the screen as I do, the scowl, the dark circles under my eyes. *The anger.*

When I was younger, this was all I wanted. I basically get paid to party and live in a perpetual state of drunkenness. I lived for the thrill.

Kat used to love it too. Years ago, when we first met and

things were different. I glance at the empty seat to my left and picture her. She used to play with the buckle on every flight. Unbuckle, buckle, unbuckle, buckle. I thought it was a nervous habit at first, but it was just due to the excitement.

She loved coming with me to events. It was what we did together. Back when everything was the way it was supposed to be.

Back when life was less complicated.

Back when we were kids and I didn't realize that life was going to catch up to me.

A huff of a sigh leaves me as I shift in my seat and look back to my computer.

I click over to the flight tab and see there are four hours remaining until we'll land in London. Four hours to sit in silence and remember each and every moment that I fucked up. Every step that I took that led me to this very hour.

I turned thirty-two four months ago, but I'm living the same life I had when we were in our twenties.

She's the one who changed.

But I'm the one who screwed up.

I run a hand down my face, trying to get the images out of my head.

She can never know, but I was a fool to think I'd hidden it from her.

There's no way out of this.

How can she love me, when she knows I'm lying to her?

How can she forgive me, for a sin she has no idea I've committed?

How can I keep her, when I don't deserve her?

CHAPTER 3

Kat

They don't understand,
Because they aren't me.
They don't know what I feel,
Or see what used to be.
How can I tell,
When they refuse to hear?
How can I refute,
When the truth is so clear?

"So this is all bullshit?" Sue asks with a tone that says she doesn't think it is as she motions to the paper. Her voice is soft, but the small coffee shop walls and my nerves makes it seem louder than it is.

"It doesn't look like it's …" I can't finish my thought, my eyes drawn to the same picture I've stared at for hours last night, and the night before.

"Well, she's all over him. There's no denying that."

"Women are always all over him." My answer comes out flat. I used to like it. I loved it even. How they'd fawn over him, desperate for Evan's attention. But he only had eyes for me.

"Why is this one any different then?" The paper hits the slick, raised surface of the coffee table as she tosses it on top and immediately digs into her large Chanel hobo bag.

It's not the first, or the second or even the third time Evan's had his name in the paper for less-than-angelic reasons.

His reputation and even his livelihood rest on the fact that he's gotten away with shit that would send most people to jail. At least he did before I met him. Now he gets paid to make sure his clients get the same fate.

Sue talks as she pulls out a tube of bright pink lipstick and a compact mirror. "Do you think he really did it this time?" she asks as if the weight of our marriage doesn't rest on my answer.

The reason this time is different is because I know there's truth to it.

It's because of how he reacts.

It's how he looks at me as if he's guilty.

"He says it's not what it looks like," I say and roll my eyes as I do, trying to downplay the pain that coils in my chest. My throat goes tight, but I'm saved by the return of Maddie.

For so many years, since I first moved here really, there's been one constant. And it's these women. Jules, my first client and New York socialite who brought us all together, isn't here. I owe her so much for helping my career take off as quickly as it did, but Jules has everything and all she really wants is companionship. I know she's getting settled into married life, but at least Maddie and Sue could meet me.

"Pumpkin spice," Maddie says as she sets a hot cup of coffee down in front of me. She doesn't look me in the eyes, like she's afraid doing even that will make me cry.

The strong scent of cinnamon smacks me in the face, but I wrap my hand around the cup, giving her a grateful smile as she takes her seat to my right. I don't like flavored coffee-I don't even like pumpkin, but I'll drink it. I desperately need the caffeine.

My gaze returns to Sue, sitting straight across from me as she returns to the conversation and says, "He says it's not what it looks like … And what does that mean?" It's not a question, it's an accusation and the two of us know it.

"What does what mean?" Maddie asks innocently.

"It means he's lying," Sue spits and folds the paper over, reading the article again. It's only a paragraph, maybe two. And it doesn't say much other than the fact that Samantha Lapour and her husband are now separated, due to an affair she had with my husband, Evan Thompson. Which is bullshit. They've been in a shitty marriage for months and they were separated long before this happened.

Maddie's expression turns hard, a warning look that would normally make me laugh considering how petite and naïve she is. "We're talking about Evan," she says under her breath. Her eyes stay on Sue and slowly Sue purses her lips and acknowledges Maddie.

The newly divorced Suzette doesn't give men a chance to explain. For good reason, too.

"It's fine," I say lowly, shaking off the emotion rocking through my body and easing the tension at the table. "There's no reason for us to get into this." I don't look at either of them, blowing on the hot coffee and reluctantly drinking it.

"Well, what do you think?" Maddie asks me and then she

picks up her own cup. The coffee shop on Madison Avenue is fairly empty, probably due to the light rain and chill of the pending fall in the air.

As the shop door opens with a small chime and the busy sounds of the street flood into the small space for a moment, I think of how to answer her.

And I don't know what to say.

I think he cheated on me.

I think he's sorry and he regrets it.

I think he loves me.

And I feel like a fool for still loving him and wanting him.

That's what I think as I look around the small coffee shop, taking in every detail of the white chair rail and tan walls. The framed photographs of abstract coffee pots and coffee beans keep my attention a little longer. I've never really noticed them before. This place is so familiar, yet I couldn't have described any of these details if someone had asked me. I've been coming here for years for work and yet I'd never cared enough to look at what was right here in front of me.

"Why would he lie to you?" Maddie asks, pulling my attention back to her. "I just can't imagine Evan doing this." My shoulders rise with a deep intake of breath as I pick at the small, square napkin on the table. I roll the tiny piece I've ripped off between my finger and thumb, watching as it crumples into a small ball.

"I don't know," I answer softly. I can feel all the overwhelming sadness and betrayal rise up and make my throat tighten as I try to come up with a response. "Maybe I'm stupid, but I can't remember him ever lying to me before." I swallow thickly and flick the tiny ball onto the table. "Not like this." Defeat drips from my words.

"Sorry," I tell them and wipe under my eyes, hating that I'm even bothering to cry. "I tried not to let it …" I can't finish. I watch as the rain batters the large glass window in the front of the shop and I internally slip my armor back on.

"Don't you dare be sorry," Sue says with a strength that pulls my attention back to her. Her blunt blonde hair sways as she leans forward, moving closer to me and speaks with an undeniable authority. "If you want to cry, cry. If you want to scream, do it. Whatever you need to do, just let it out."

Maddie nods her head in my periphery, but I can't do the same.

What if I want to deal with it by falling into his arms and letting him lie to me? I know it's not okay, yet that's all I want. I want him to fight for me. I want him to love me. I want to forgive him, even if he won't admit what he's done.

And that makes me a coward and a pathetic excuse for a modern-day woman, doesn't it?

The snide thought makes me turn my attention back to the dreary state of affairs outside. The clouds have set in and the sky quickly turns dark.

"This is shit weather for our first meeting," I say out loud, not really meaning to.

"Way to turn the conversation," Sue says as she picks up her coffee cup and takes a sip. Her light blue eyes stare back at me as she drinks and it almost makes me laugh. Almost.

"So you're meeting your client here?" Maddie asks, gracefully accepting my invitation to talk about anything else. I've never loved her more than in this very moment.

I nod my head, still not trusting myself to speak and take a drink from the cup in front of me. I forgot it was pumpkin spice and I nearly spit it out, surprised by the flavor, but then I swallow it down. It's not so bad.

Maddie pulls her dark brown, curly hair over her shoulder and scrunches her nose as she takes in my expression. "You don't like pumpkin?" she asks, raising a brow in disbelief.

"It's okay," I answer her straight-faced and Sue erupts with a laugh that catches the attention of an elderly couple behind us. Her good humor is infectious and I find myself smiling. This is what I need. To talk and think about something else. Anything else.

"I'll get you something else," Maddie offers as Sue starts to speak. "Just regular?"

"Well, you look professional," Sue says with a nod.

"Thanks, but don't worry about it, Maddie. It's good." I wave off her concern and take another sip. "I just need some caffeine."

"Trouble sleeping?" Maddie asks and I just nod my head once and turn back to the cup, hating that the conversation is moving backward, but I can't help it.

"I just wish I had ..." I can't finish the sentence and I struggle to come up with something to say as I push the hair from my face and try to remember what I want. I haven't got a clue. "I wish I had my life together," I practically whisper, but they hear and I know they do.

"You do have your life together. You're an established publisher. An entrepreneur and a hard worker."

I have work. Yes.

But not a damn thing else. Not enough to hold on to a life I somehow strayed from.

The thought makes me miserable, and I focus on the coffee again, drinking it down as if it'll save me. When I set it down, I notice how empty it is, tapping the bottom of it against the table. I'm going to need another. I'll get it myself though. I push away from the table slightly. "I'm going to grab another. At this rate it'll be empty before Jacob gets here."

"Oh, Jacob," Sue says his name with a hint of something I can't describe in her voice. A devilish smile grows on her face and it makes me roll my eyes. Of all the girls, Sue's the one who gets over one man by getting under another. And she's given the advice freely to our tight group of friends. I can practically feel her elbow in my ribs.

"Yes, Jacob," I mock the way she said it, feeling irritable and like a bitch, but it only makes Sue smile.

"Well I hope he's a good distraction for you," Sue tells me and slides her bag off her lap and onto her shoulder.

"Work is always a good distraction." My tone destroys the bit of lightness. "I'm good at burying myself in it." The girls are quiet as my words sit stale in the air. It's part of the reason my marriage is tainted. I don't have to say it out loud and they don't have to tell me. Everyone already knows it.

"I read the book you gave me," Maddie says, changing the subject back to Jacob Scott. "I looked him up online, too," she adds as a smile spreads across her lips and her cheeks brighten with a blush. She scoots to the back of her seat and holds her cup in both hands, gladly taking the attention off of me. "He's cute," she says with a smile. My left brow raises as I watch her pink cheeks turn brighter. *Little miss innocent.*

"Is he now?" Sue answers her and the two share a look as Maddie nods.

"Want me to put in a good word for you?" I ask her and reach into my Kate Spade satchel for my laptop and notebook, setting them up on the table as Sue stands and puts on her jacket. There's no way Maddie would actually make a move. She's so sheltered and inexperienced. There's no way I'd let someone like Jacob near her. I'll play along though. "You can always stay and wait for him to get here?" I offer jokingly. "Or maybe leave something behind and have to come back for it?"

She doesn't answer, merely shakes her head and slides off her seat to join Sue.

"I wouldn't want to intrude," she finally says and then

walks over to give me a hug. Even in her heels, I still sit a little higher at the bar-height table as she embraces me.

I half expect her to say something in my ear, to tell me it'll be alright or that Evan's made a mistake. But she doesn't say a word until she lets me go. "I'm just a call away," she says with a chipper tone that wouldn't clue in anyone around us that I'd need to call her because my life is falling apart.

"Same here, darling," Sue says and then the two walk off. Sue's heels click noticeably louder as she opens the door. But the chime sounds just the same as when we first walked in here.

"Thanks for coming, guys," I tell them and smile as they leave me here alone.

But the smile doesn't reflect anything I truly feel.

And nothing's changed.

CHAPTER 4

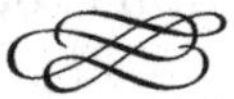

Evan

It was a mistake; I can't change the past.
I don't want this to be, the pain is steadfast.
I haven't paid for my sins, how long can I run?
In time, the truth will be revealed-
I'll be dead and it will have won.

Berkeley Square in London feels the same as it has for years. The crisp air and old trees that tower over the park. The black iron and white stone that speak to the history of this place. The dark, narrow alleys and the nightlife tucked away in the shadows of this city are what make my blood heat and my foot tap anxiously on the floorboard of the car.

It's always given me a rush to come here. There are a

number of cities I'm fond of, cities that are playgrounds for the rich and where the best parties are had. Los Angeles, San Francisco, New York City of course. But London is one of the best. There's something to be said about being away from your normal life and getting to unwind in a city you don't have any obligations to stay in.

The cabbie clears his throat and his accent greets me as he tries to make small talk. I give him a nod and as many one-word answers as it takes to make it clear he doesn't need to fill the time with needless conversation. I'm not interested.

I rub the sleep from my eyes, feeling more and more exhausted as we pass the park, the dark green landscape fading from sight and rows of homes taking the place of the public areas.

I've felt comfortable here for years. It's a constant go-to for the PR company and I've been sent here to look after clients practically every year. But as the sky turns gray and the rain starts to spit on the roof, the welcoming feeling leaves me, and I'm left empty. Brought back to the present and brooding on how much the past has fucked me over.

The cab takes a left onto Hay Hill and I pass an old townhome where I used to crash. I've had so many close calls here. I was too much of a hothead, always looking for a thrill and pushing my luck further and further.

The cabbie comes to a stop before I'm ready. The memories play over and over in the back of my head of all the years I spent wasted. I can still feel the crunch of bone from the last fight I got into not three blocks from here.

"Here we are," the cabbie says, turning in his seat, but before he can say anything else, I jam the cash into his hand and grab my bags on my own.

"Have a good day, sir," I hear him call out as I shut the door, the patter of rain already soaking the collar on the back of my neck.

I have to walk with my head down to keep the rain from hitting me in the face. The door opens easily and I drag my luggage in, tossing it to the right side where the coatrack and desk are meant to greet clients. The historical condo is converted into an office space. It's blocks from the nightlife and blends in with the community. A perfect location for client drop-off.

The high ceilings and intricate molding make the already expensive building feel that much wealthier. It's all shades of white and cream, without an actual color in sight, save for the bright neon sticky note on top of a stack of papers that's sitting on the edge of the welcome desk.

Sterile, but rich.

"You were supposed to tell me when you landed." I hear James' voice before I see him, his heavy steps echoing in the expansive room.

"I did," I tell him flatly, not bothering to take out my phone and check. I'm sure I did and he ignored it. That seems to have been his preference for the last two weeks. The air about him has changed; ever since that night, things have been tense between us. Like we're in a silent war, each waiting for the other to show weakness.

I'm not interested in this shit. The only thing I give a damn about is my Kat. And keeping her safe from the crossfire.

"I didn't get it," he says, stopping in front of me in the foyer. He has to tilt his head slightly to look me in the eye since he's a few inches shorter.

I shrug as if it doesn't matter, not bothering to confirm or deny whether a text was sent. "Well I'm here now," I answer him as I slide off my jacket, soaked with the rain from outside and hang it on the coatrack.

"You look like shit," he tells me and an asymmetric grin tilts my lips up.

"Thanks," I say and face him, running a hand over my

hair and wiping off the rain on my jeans. "I'd say I feel better than I look, but that'd be a lie."

I've known James a long time, nearly a decade and I expect him to ask why, even though he already knows. I anticipate him starting the conversation, but instead he says nothing. Avoiding the obvious and walking down the hallway of the townhouse.

My feet move on their own, following him even though adrenaline courses faster in my blood. It makes me feel sick to not talk about it. To not clear the air.

"Whiskey?" he asks me as he pours himself a glass on the right side of a converted dining room. It's more of a bar now with a long plank of cedar serving as a makeshift counter in the back of the room. The recessed lighting hits the bottles of clear and amber liquids and creates an intimate feel in the room. The only exception to this being a bar is a humidifier full of cigars on the left and a pair of dark leather wingback chairs on either side of it.

"Kane Buchan," James says and hands me a folder. I'm sure it's filled with the same shit that was emailed to me. I've got the profile memorized. He was the lead singer in a rock band from the Bronx. They had one smash hit and then he split from the rest of them. He decided to go separate ways because he was too good for the band. Most said it was his ego, but it turns out he was right. Three hits on the top charts and now he's a client.

They all want the same. To flaunt their wealth, get drunk or high. Fuck whoever they want.

"He said something about going to Annabel's tonight," James tells me and I nod my head. I've been there a time or two. It's exclusive and ridiculously overpriced, so of course an up-and-coming star wants to be seen there.

They're all the same. I can see exactly how the night's going to play out. I just have to keep it clean enough so there are no problems.

"Did you even hear what I said?" James asks me in a raised voice laced with irritation.

"Annabel's," I tell him as I look him in the eyes and hope he was still going on about the club.

"No, I said he's married so make sure there are no pictures if he does something stupid."

"I know," I say.

"He's staying a few days, maybe less depending on what his agent wants. Just keep an eye on him, show him a good time-" He's pissing me off. Treating me like a new hire and nothing more.

"I know what to do," I retort and cut James off deliberately. "I've been here before."

I've had days to think of how to approach this, but I still hesitate to get everything off my chest.

He huffs a response, something like disbelief and then grabs the tumbler of whiskey from the table. The ice clinks as he takes a sip and then holds it in front of him.

"Buchan's agent doesn't need any more press other than what they've hired."

"I want you to know," I start as I stare him in the eyes, forcing him to listen to what I'm telling him. "I think it was a setup." Maybe I'm paranoid, but I don't give a fuck. I have to tell someone. And I'm sure as shit not going to Samantha. "It was an accident, but it just doesn't seem right. Something's off."

He shrugs and says, "I don't give a shit."

"I do." My words come out hard and bitter, but James is already walking away from me. I know if I move an inch, if I even breathe, I'll beat the piss out of him for leaving this all on me. And risk everything.

CHAPTER 5

Kat

Saying goodbye is hard, meaning it is harder,
It's futile to deny what I truly desire.
To fuel the need that runs in my blood,
To tread the fear and not drown in the flood.
I can try to fight it, I can try to run,
But the damage has only just begun.

My eyes feel bloodshot. They burn just from the cool air as I finally sit back down in my office. I'm always here. I never leave this room unless I have to.

And when I do I bring my laptop with me.

Workaholic is a word for it. I'm not sure that even does it justice. I gave up everything for this.

It's why I came to New York.

It's why I spent years in the publishing industry, making contacts and creating a brand that's recognizable. But I do it on my own.

While Evan stayed the same, and carried on with a life that was a fun distraction, I've buried myself in work. Growing farther and farther apart from my husband.

Ignored friends ... at least I didn't have family to ignore. Other than Evan.

I rub my eyes again and try to soothe them, but the darkness is all I can see. It begs me to sleep.

I desperately need it. I can't even read an email right. My meeting with Jacob is *next* week. I spent an entire hour sitting mindlessly in the coffee shop on my own before I bothered to check the time and date.

At least the coffee was comforting. But the rain was coming down in sheets, and any sense of ease was gone by the time I dragged my ass back home to an empty townhouse.

My shoulders rise and fall as I take another look at the screen. The black and white is too harsh and I almost shut the laptop down and give in to sleep, but my phone goes off, scaring the shit out of me.

Evan.

It's my first thought and I hate how my heart sinks when I see it's not him. It's his father.

In my contact list, it still says Evan's parents' house.

It's the house phone in Evan's family home.

Marie gave the number to me the night I first saw her, so she could call me about next Sunday's dinner, all those years ago. Every time I see it, *Evan's parents' house,* I'm reminded that only Henry remains.

It's not a reminder I welcome. Just the same as the reminder of my own parents' sudden death in a car crash.

That's something Evan and I had in common, both of us losing our loved ones so quickly. He still has his father at least, but I've had no one for most of my life.

We'd only been seeing each other for a few months when I got the first call from this number. I was expecting for it to be Marie, but it wasn't his mother making the call, it was Evan because his cell phone had died.

He told me he couldn't make it to our date, and the first thought I had was that he was breaking up with me. It wasn't until he apologized that I realized it was something else.

He couldn't hold it together on the phone. His voice shook and his sentences were short. I'll never forget that feeling in my chest, like I knew everything was over and there was nothing I could do about it.

There was something in his voice that I recognized. It was how you sound when you're trying to convince someone else you're okay, but you're not. I knew it well.

I got tired of having to convince people. People who didn't bother to get to know me, because I was just the sad girl at the end of the block. The *poor child* everyone talked about.

It was why I moved to New York. Living in the small town where your family died isn't a healthy place for someone who just wants to feel like there's something else in this world other than the past.

But for Evan it wasn't what had happened, it was the inevitable that brought him to his weakest moment.

I insisted on seeing him and meeting him at his parents' place and even though I thought he'd object, he didn't. He'd never been so passive toward anything like he was that night.

Evan's only cried twice since I've known him.

That night after his mother had finally gone to bed and we went back to his childhood bedroom. And nineteen days later, when she was put in the ground.

"Henry," I answer the phone as if nothing's wrong. My voice is peppy and full of life, even though it's nearly 10 p.m. and I feel nothing but dead inside.

I squint at the clock on the computer and wonder why he's calling so late. "Is everything alright?" I ask him, my heart beating slower and a deep fear of loss settling in.

"My favorite daughter-in-law," Henry greets me and it makes a soft smile bring the corners of my lips up. I even feel the warmth from it.

"Your *only* daughter-in-law," I correct him, picking at a bit of fuzz on the sleeve of my shirt.

"Still my favorite," he says and I give him the laugh that he's after, even if it is a little short and quiet.

"What's going on?" I ask him and rest my elbow on the desk, chin in my hand. I absently minimize the document on my screen and clear out all my tabs, checking my email one last time as Henry talks.

"I just wanted to check on you, make sure everything's good."

Again, I get the sense that something's off. "That's sweet

of you," I answer him but before I can say everything's fine, he beats me to the real reason he called.

"You two alright?" he asks.

"Yeah," I lie and instantly feel like shit. But what am I going to tell him? That right now, I don't know if my marriage to his son will last? That I'm falling apart and I have no idea how to make this better? That his son is a liar and I hate him for the pain he's putting me through?

"I spoke to Evan and he said he's not sure about the holidays coming up," Henry says as if he's baiting me. And he is.

The screen of my laptop dims, ridding the room of any light so I hit the space bar and bring it back to life.

"It's a bit away, but," I pause and swallow, not knowing how to word it. I don't have family, so it's not as if I can use them as an excuse. "Work may be a little much," I finally breathe the words slowly, giving him a lie I'm sure he knows is exactly that.

"He said you're going through something." There's no bullshit in his voice as he adds, "That you two aren't doing the best."

"Did he?" I ask weakly. It's a betrayal. That's how I feel hearing that Evan's told his father what we're going through. It makes the crack in my heart that much deeper.

It's not fair that he welcomes so much attention. I don't need the judgment. Because I don't want their opinions. I don't want them to know we're flawed. I just want us whole again. I wish no one knew so I could silently be the weak wife I am. The one willing to turn a blind eye for the unfaithful man she loves more than herself.

"I don't want to talk about it, Henry," I tell him as my eyes close. I can tell the computer has gone into sleep mode again and this time I don't hit the keys to bring it back to life. The darkness is too comforting.

"I just want you to know I'm here for you," Henry says clearly into the phone. "You're my daughter," he adds and it breaks my composure.

I push away from the desk, the chair legs catching on the rug and nearly tipping over. I walk slowly to the door and then to my bedroom, the phone still to my ear, each step trying to keep it all down. Just moving through the motions and trying to be numb to it.

"Thank you," I tell him, breathing the words as I lean against the bedroom door, closing it and almost tell him, he's like a father to me.

Almost, but when we do get a divorce, Henry won't be

there for me. It doesn't matter what he says. It doesn't matter that I'll be alone, because that's how I've been most of my life anyway.

"I love you and I'm sorry you two are going through this." I let Henry's words echo in my head.

He's not the only one who's sorry.

CHAPTER 6

Evan

Years of the same can't be erased or denied.
The past is unforgiving to a wounded pride.
The choices I made will stay to the end.
I'll pay for my sins, it's a truth that won't bend.

The music pounds away, the bass so loud it vibrates my chest. The nightclub is pitch black between bright colorful lights that flash in beat with the music.

"Another!" Kane's friend Mikey yells on my left, a little too close to my ear for comfort, a little too loud. But I just smile and pretend to take another swig of my beer.

Another time in my life, I'd actually be drinking. I like the feel that I get on the right side of a heavy buzz. That light headiness where you still have control, but not a damn thing matters. That's the place I craved to be for so long, but not anymore.

It's been a few hours and so far the job's been easy. Kane and his friends are trashed and he's having the time of his life. They're saddled up to the bar with a few women. One in particular for Kane, which has me on edge and keeping an eye out for the telltale glow of a cell phone in the air, ready to capture a snapshot.

She's the blonde closest to Kane, Christi she said her name was, and the loudest by far. The more she drinks, the louder she gets, and the closer to Kane.

According to the paperwork, the tall, loudmouthed blonde is his type and it wouldn't be the first time he's strayed from his wife. Fame and fortune tend to do it. I've seen it too many times to count.

And Kat thinks this is the type of shit I do. The thought makes me sick to my stomach, a scowl marring my face and I know it. I can't change it so I raise the beer to my lips and take a long swig of it, nearly draining the bottle. She's never questioned me before, but last night she let out shit I had no idea about. Insecurities and accusations that made me feel like less of a man.

I can't blame her, can I? Not when I have secrets. Not

when I can't look her in the eyes and tell her I haven't fucked up.

A strong grip on my arm rouses me from my thoughts.

"Can you get me something?" Kane asks, siding up beside me. The smell of whiskey assaults me and I almost push him away.

Just like Mikey, he's a little too close as he slurs his request to the point where I can't tell what he's saying.

"What are you looking for?" I ask him and stare at the shine of the half-empty glass bottles of liquor lining the bar.

"Something a little stronger," he says as he tilts his head and then tries to be subtle, putting his hand to his nose and sniffling. Cocaine.

I hesitate and waver on my answer. Luckily, I don't have to respond. Instead a loud, high-pitched voice on my right screams out, "We've got absinthe!" Apparently the blonde was eavesdropping. Surprise, surprise. Her talons are gripped tight on Kane and I know she's going to stay within hearing range until we're out of here, just like she's been doing since she found out who he is. She's leaning over a barstool, her breasts on full display and when I look back at Kane, the only thing he's looking at is her chest.

"Never had it," Kane says too low and the blonde screams, practically in my ear, "What?!"

I back away a bit, getting out from between the two of them and wait for him to agree. I know he will. She's got him wrapped around her finger. I'll do it with a smile on my face and babysit this fucker. I used to think of this differently. This shit used to be fun. But it wasn't like *this,* was it?

It doesn't take more than one girly laugh from the blonde to convince Kane that absinthe is good enough and that we should all head to her place.

It's two blocks down and up a set of iron rails to get to the apartment. The sidewalk's still wet and this late at night, there's no one on the streets. Just a bunch of drunk assholes stumbling on their way home. We fit in perfectly. I keep my eyes ahead, but occasionally look back and in all directions casually.

I follow them as Kane and his friend follow the group of women. There are three of them, two blondes and a dark brunette with curls, each barely covered in skimpy club-wear as they grip the railing to the apartment stairs and laugh their way as they stumble up in heels that clank against the iron grid floor.

Kane's hands are all over Christi, moving from her hips to her ass as he walks behind her. Mikey's into the other blonde and the brunette's checked out, only interested in smoking weed and getting trashed.

At one point, I thought this was fun.

I tolerated the attention and flirting, but after a few minutes of ignoring the women, they always lost interest and moved on to the next. Somehow it always gave me a thrill, but there's nothing about this night that gives me any pleasure. I just want to get back to Kat and make her take it all back. Make her forget what happened and remind her why we're meant to be together. Remind her why she's mine.

I don't want this life anymore. I can't take this shit.

Not when it makes Kat doubt me and what we have. Rightfully so.

As the girls laugh and the door opens, I take my phone out of my pocket, peeking up to make sure none of the girls have theirs out.

No pictures.

That's my second concern. The first is getting Kane and getting out of here. He's had a good time; he'll remember enough of it at least. I'm not interested in being here any longer than I have to be.

I'm distracted for only a moment. Half a second, but the

moment I stop watching these girls, one of them breaks rule number one.

The second the blonde on the right pulls out her iPhone, turning and posing with her friend and Kane in the background, I snatch it from her. She gasps and tries to grab it back like this is a game and I'm making a move on her. Her smile widens and she lets out a small laugh, again trying to snatch it from me.

It takes her a minute to realize no matter how much she pulls on my arm and makes that girlish cry, I have no intention of giving it back.

"No pictures," I tell her simply, my voice low and admonishing and my expression hard. I don't have time for this shit or her antics. She knows what she's doing and it's not cute or funny.

I force myself to stare into her drunken hazel gaze until she looks down and then holds out her hand for it. The flirtation completely gone. "I get it," she snaps.

I place the phone in her palm after I shut it off, and she huffs like I'm an asshole. I can see her biting her tongue wanting to tell me off and I can't really blame her. She wouldn't be the first. I've been slapped more times than I know. Mostly by women. Years of doing this have led to plenty of fights and unfortunate events.

I've beaten the shit out of assholes.

Called doctors and paid with cash for them to come to hotel rooms.

I've paid off cops, bouncers, bookies. Shit, I've seen it all, done it all. And I'm tired of this shit.

The bright green of the absinthe catches my eye as the blonde I just pissed off brings it to the coffee table. I watch as she sets it in the center and lines up three shot glasses before going back to the small kitchen only ten feet away to grab more out of a drawer.

Kane's in the middle of the sofa, draping both arms across the back of it as Christi and the brunette cuddle up next to him. The sounds of them laughing and Kane saying something low as they huddle closer to him are barely on my mind as I turn my focus back to my phone.

I text the driver and let him know I'm going to need the car in about thirty minutes and send him the address.

It takes fifteen minutes for the alcohol to hit their systems. Heavy pours and three shots each will have them all out on their asses. Normally I'd feel bad cutting their party short, but I don't give a shit. All I can think about is Kat.

I need to get back to her.

I plaster a smile on my face and roll up my sleeves. "Let me get it, doll," I say as I make my way to the kitchen. "You sit back and relax," I tell the blonde and take the bottle from her hands. I'll be pouring the second round while they're throwing back the first. She gives me a flirtatious smirk. "I knew you weren't all asshole," she says and then sits on her knees next to the coffee table. Too close, too presumptuous.

"You had it right the first time," I tell her as I fill all six glasses and pass them out. "Let's do a couple rounds and get this party started."

CHAPTER 7

Kat

I'm stronger than this. I deserve so much more.
They're the words I breathe, then collapse on the floor.
My eyes close tight, the tears trapped, my lungs still.
I can't speak the truth; I can't fight the chill.
I'm stronger than this, I'll tell myself till I rot.
But I know I'm a liar, and I know that I'm not.

Evan never texts me when he's working, but he did tonight and I can't take my eyes away from my phone because of it. My body's still and my focus is nonexistent when it comes to work. He messaged me. He reached out to me. I can't explain why it makes my cracked heart splinter even deeper. Maybe I wish he'd just be cruel and not try or not care. It hurts so much more to think that he's trying.

I've learned over the years not to expect him to message me or call, not to worry. To trust him and to look for a message in the morning. He always messaged in the morning. I've always thought it was cute how he'd text me to tell me good morning, even if he was only just then getting into bed.

But it's 2 a.m. in London, and my phone's lit on the desk with a message from him.

I was finally getting some work done. Focusing and managing to write up some feedback and create a marketing tactic for a client. Half of me doesn't want to answer him. I don't want to look and go back into the black hole of self-pity. But I can't resist.

My hands inch toward it, the need to see what he has to say overriding the anger and the sadness. The need to be wanted by him and to feel loved winning out over my dignity.

I hate it when you're mad at me.

I stare at his message, feeling my heart squeeze tight. My fingers hesitate over the keys as I read it again and again. Before I can respond, another message comes through.

Forgive me.

And that's the crux of the situation.

Forgive you for what exactly? I message him back without even thinking. Whatever he's hiding is bad, I know it is. I can feel it deep down in my core. Whatever he's done is enough to ruin us.

But we were already ruined. In my gut, I can feel it. We've grown apart. We're different people now. *We don't belong together.* We never did really.

I have to get up and move. Even if it's just to walk through the house. I'm only in a baggy shirt and a pair of socks. I wore the shirt to sleep last night and I should really shower and get dressed. It's a rule I've had since I started working from home.

I dress as if I'm going into the office. Well, I used to. Right now I just don't have the energy.

Evan sends two texts, one right after the other as I walk to the kitchen.

We can work through this.

I love you.

I only glance at them before putting the phone down on the counter and heading straight to the fridge for the wine.

There's only half a glass left in the dark red bottle, but it'll have to do.

I glance at the clock as I sip it. It's after 9 p.m. I've barely slept, barely worked and I'm still in my pajamas from last night. But at least I'm drinking from a clean glass.

It only takes one sip before I just ask him what's on my mind.

I just don't understand why you won't tell me what you did.

Won't tell you what? he texts back and it pisses me off.

"Does he think I'm stupid?" I mutter beneath my breath as my blood boils. The anger is only an ounce stronger than the pain.

Don't treat me like this. I text him back, feeling weak. I'm practically begging him. *I deserve better.*

I down the wine after sending the last line. I don't know exactly what it is I deserve. Him telling me the truth. Him confiding in me. Or a better husband altogether.

As I grip the neck of the last bottle of red wine on the rack and bring it back to the kitchen, I realize this is how women feel when they stay in these marriages.

They'd rather be told a sweet little lie and believe it, than face the truth.

Right now, it's exactly what I want. Just lie to me. Tell me there's nothing that happened. That it's blown out of proportion. *That it was just a kiss.* Yes, that one. That last one. I could forgive it, but better yet, I could believe it.

The barstool legs scratch on the floor as I scoot it under my butt and sit down to uncork the new bottle.

I just want him to come home. Tell me everything is fine and make up something that's easy to forgive.

A bottle of wine and a refilled glass in front of me, I go back to the beginning. Back to when I was stronger and I actually had self-respect.

Back when I knew better.

The memory and the wine are the only things I have to keep myself company for the rest of the night, because Evan doesn't text me back.

Six years ago

The wind blows in my face, mixed with the stale summer heat as I pull into the corner store parking lot in Brooklyn. It's late and the hustle and bustle of New York has waned, but the nightlife on this side of the city is only getting started.

Some would say it's the bad part of town, but others say it's the fun part. I guess it depends on what circles you run in. I'm new to New York and struggling to find where I belong. The lights and sophistication are what I came here for, but making it here isn't so easily achieved.

I'm slow to step on the brakes and pull into the last spot on the far right against the curb that lines the sidewalk to the small store. I've only been here a few times, either needing to stop for gas or a quick bite to eat on my way to or from work on the west side of the city.

Several cars line the front of the store and a few men head inside as I pull up. They vary from obviously expensive to looking like they're falling apart. The vehicles, that is.

I notice the men, and they notice me. Averting their gaze, I turn down my radio and put my car in park.

I mind my business and everyone around me seems to do the same. In the city that never sleeps, there's always something happening. And I'm not interested in a lot of those somethings.

I grab my purse and keys in the same hand and open the car door to step out with no time to waste, but my eyes glance back to the cars and straight into a man's gaze.

Not just any man, a man exuding power and confidence, along with defiance. Although he's wearing a simple shirt and faded dark jeans, the way he wears them makes me think they were made to be fitted to his muscular body. He's hot as hell, and given the way he looks at me, he could be a temptation the devil made just for me.

My driver's side door shuts with a loud bang as I stand there caught in the heat in his eyes. He's leaning against the hood of a car, I would guess it's his, a shiny black Mercedes that illuminates the light from the store in its slick reflection. The windows are rolled up and tinted so dark it's hard to see the interior. As my eyes move back to the man, my movements are slowed and I grip my keys tighter.

He doesn't stop looking, taking me in and letting his eyes follow along my body. He obviously wants me to know that he's watching me.

My breathing picks up and I subconsciously pull my dress down just slightly, smoothing out the cherry red pleats and wishing I hadn't been wearing it all day. I take one step and the click of my heels keeps time as I walk forward, knowing I have to pass him on my way in.

I can't help that my eyes flicker over to his as I grip my purse strap and settle it in place. His tanned skin is pulled taut and smooth over his muscular frame and decorated with ink. Tattoos travel from his collarbone down, peeking out from the crisp white cotton shirt and leaving a trail of intricate designs all the way down to his wrists. I'm too far away to see what they say or what they are. I know if he were in a suit, the tattoos would be hidden, but something tells me he's proud to have them on full display.

"What are you up to?" he asks me and catches me off guard.

"I don't think that's any of your business," I tell him easily, although I don't know how, swaying a little from side to side in a flirtatious way I didn't intend. My body can't help but be attracted to him. To want to know how his tattooed skin feels against my fingertips.

There's a scar over his left eyebrow and it's subtle, but even from this distance I notice it. As his deep, rough chuckle fills the night air and drowns out the other sounds of the city, I find myself wondering how he got it.

"A man can wonder though," he says, making a hot blush creep slowly into my cheeks. I bite down on my lower lip, but that doesn't stop the shy smile from showing. I have to stop and give him the attention he's looking for as he leans forward, holding me captive to whatever's on his mind.

"You're pretty, you know that?" he asks me and I roll my eyes. He makes me feel things I haven't before. Even if I know this flirtation isn't just for me, that he's simply playing with me, I still enjoy it. I crave it even.

"Sure, and you're not too bad looking either." I enjoy the flirting, the attention. At least coming from him.

He splays a hand over his heart and cocks his head as he says,

"Well thank you, beautiful, I aim for not bad." This time I'm the one laughing, a short, soft laugh as I kick the bottom of my heels against the ground and stare at them for a moment, readying myself to say goodbye and end his bout of teasing. I don't trust myself not to say anything and instead I just wave and carry on, expecting him to do the same.

"You didn't answer me," he calls out after I take a few steps. "What are you doing out here so late?" he asks. It's forward of him and I usually despise that, but instead I savor the challenge in his voice. Something about it tells me he thinks I'm already his. And that ownership makes my blood that much hotter.

I know I shouldn't give him any information at all, but I find myself telling him the truth before I can stop myself. "I'm hungry and overworked. So I stopped to grab a bite to eat."

"You're getting your dinner from here?" he asks, gesturing to the store and I nod. "A woman like you should be taken out, not eating dinner from the gas station."

A woman like you, *plays over and over in my head. He doesn't know what type of woman I am. "You don't even know my name," I tell him, the half smile and challenge firm on my expression.*

He nods and grins, flashing me a cocky, asymmetrical smile as he replies, "Don't make me guess."

I chew on my lip for a moment, rocking from side to side. He's bad news and I'm flirting with fire ... but I love the thrill. I can't deny it. "It's Kat," I tell him and a smile is slow to form on his face. One of complete satisfaction, as if hearing my name is the best thing that's happened to him all night.

"I'm Evan," he says and I taste his name on the tip of my tongue, nearly whispering it. "Let me take you to dinner, Kat," he suggests with an easiness I don't like. I wonder how many times that's worked for him before.

"I'm not your type," I tell him, intentionally looking past him at the bars that wrap around the glass door to the convenience store. I just need a late night snack to hold me over till morning. That's all this little errand was supposed to turn into.

"I don't think you should tell me what is and isn't my type," he tells me although it comes out playful. "You might be surprised," he adds.

I clear my throat and try to breathe evenly, wanting this flirting session to end so I can get back to work. I have to admit the attention is very much needed though. And the desire in his eyes looks genuine.

"Sorry, Charlie, didn't mean to upset you," I tell him with a playful pout as I walk past him.

"It's Evan," he repeats his name and that makes a wicked grin play at my lips, "and you're wrong," he tells me with a seriousness I wasn't expecting. His tone is hard and when I turn

around to face him fully, finally taking a step onto the curb, he's no longer sitting on the hood of the Mercedes. He takes a few strides across the asphalt parking lot and stops in front of me as I ask, "Wrong about what?"

He's taller standing up, more intimidating too and his shoulders seem broader, stronger. Even his subtle moves, as he brushes his jaw with his rough fingers and licks his lower lip again, are dominating. He glances to the left and right before opening his mouth again and letting that deep, rough voice practically whisper between us.

"You're wrong that you aren't my type and that I'm not your type."

My body sways on its own, the compliment making my body feel hotter than it already is in the hot summer night. Someone behind me exits the store, the telltale jingle of the bells and the whoosh of air-conditioning reminding me that I'm supposed to be in and out of this store. Reminding me that Evan isn't a part of my to-do list tonight.

"I never said you weren't my type," I say and my voice comes out sultry, laced with the desire I feel coursing in my blood. I try to hold his gaze, but the fire and intensity swirling in his dark eyes makes me back down.

I can try to be tough all I want, but he's a bad boy through and through and I should know better.

"Good to know," he says with a cocky undertone that makes my eyes whip up to his. I half expect him to blow me off now that his ego's been fed. But he licks his lower lip and my eyes are drawn to the motion, imagining how it'd feel to have his lips on every inch of my skin. "Come out with me tonight," he tells me. As if I don't have anything better to do. As if he can just command me to do what he wants.

"Sorry ... Evan. I can't tonight," I tell him and turn back around, shifting my purse on my shoulder and ready to go about my business.

"Tomorrow night then," he raises his voice so I can hear him as I wrap my hand around the handle and pull the door open. Again the chill of the store greets me, but this time it's unwanted.

I'm very aware of what this man could do to me. He's the type to pin you down as he takes you how he wants you and doesn't stop until you're screaming. And I can't lie, just that thought alone makes me desperate to say yes.

He takes another step closer as I stand with the door wide open and hesitate to answer. Shoving his hands into his pockets, he manages a shrug as if it's a casual question.

"Just one date," he adds as he looks at me with a raised brow and his version of puppy dog eyes. It's enough to force a smile on my face.

"And what am I supposed to do? Meet you here at ten?" I ask him.

"How about at Jean-Georges in Central Park?" he asks and I'm taken aback. It's an expensive place and my eyes glance back to his car, to his ripped body and tattooed skin. There's something about the air that follows him that screams he's no good. The danger in the way he looks at me is so tempting though.

"I just want to feed you," he adds as the time ticks slowly by and a short, older man with salt and pepper hair walks out of the exit, stealing our attention and making my hand slip slightly on the handle.

I chew on the inside of my cheek. The answer is an easy one. No. Simple as that. He's a bad boy who only wants one thing, but I can't deny that I want it too.

I SAID YES.

To the date, and then again a year later to marrying him.

That initial yes, pushed through my lips by an undeniable attraction, was my first mistake on a list of too fucking many.

All because I can't tell him no.

CHAPTER 8

Evan

"I'm sorry." I can say the words,
But I can't take what's happened back.
What's more to do? What's more to say?
There's nothing left but attack after attack.
I don't want to fight; I don't want to run.
I only want you until my life is done.
Forgive me please, but don't ask what for.
I don't deserve you anymore.

I try to shut the front door softly, as quietly as I can so I don't wake Kat up if she's passed out. Our townhouse is small and the walls are thin so you can hear everything in here. I stop in the foyer, setting the duffle bag and my luggage down and look at the living room.

The room is mostly gray, just like the city. There's a paned glass mirror above the long sofa and black and white accents everywhere. I hated that mirror from the moment we got it, but Kat loved it so I never said a word.

My eyes scan the room in the faint light from the city that's shining through the gap in the curtains.

Five years of marriage, six of creating this place together.

Each piece of furniture is a memory. The wine rack that we purchased was the first thing we bought together. The gray sofa with removable pillows was a fight I lost. I didn't want the cushions to be removable, because they always end up sagging, but Kat insisted the brand was quality.

The plush cushions still look like they did in the store, and I wonder if she was right or if it's just because we don't even sit on the damn thing.

I'm never here and she's always working. What's the point of it?

The bitter thought makes me kick the duffle bag out of my way and head past the living room and dining room, straight to the stairs so I can get to bed and lie down with Kat. It's been almost a week since I've slept in the same room as her and I refuse to let that go on for another night. I pause to look at the photos on the wall.

They're all in black and white, the way Kat likes her décor. All but one, the largest in the very center. It's also the only one that's not staged.

She's leaning toward me, and her lips look so red as she's midlaugh, holding a crystal glass of champagne and wrapping her fingers around my forearm. Her eyes are on whoever was giving a speech. I don't remember who it was or what they said, but I can still hear her laugh. It's the most beautiful sound.

She was so happy on our wedding day. I thought she'd be stressed and worried, but it was like a weight was lifted and the sweetest version of her was given to me that day. There's nothing but love there.

My eyes are on her in that picture, with a smile on my face and pride in my eyes.

I tear my gaze away and keep walking, feeling the weight of everything press down on my shoulders. I'm exhausted and like the childish fool I am, I wish I could just go to sleep and this would all be a dream.

I want to go back to when we first married. Before we both got caught up in work and decided to live separate lives. Before I fucked up.

I just want to go back to that day.

As I pass the open office door I hear the clicking of the computer keyboard. So many nights I've come home to this, so many mornings I've woken up to it. She's always in this room, which is a shame. There's hardly any light, or anything at all in the room. File cabinets, papers, a shredder and a desk. There's not a hint of the woman Kat is in this room.

I guess it's the same as the living room, but at least there's a classic elegance there. It's nothing but cold in her office.

"Hey babe," I say softly and Kat ignores me.

I clear my throat and speak louder. "I'm home," I tell her and again, I get nothing from Kat, just the steady clicks. There's an empty wine glass and two bottles on the floor by her feet.

Maybe she's a little drunk, maybe she has her earplugs in too, but still, she'd hear me.

My teeth grind together as I grip the handle of the door harder. She deserves better. Yeah, I know she does. And this is the shit I deserve, but I don't want it. I won't go down without fighting for what I want.

The standing lamp in the corner of her office is on, but it's not enough to brighten the room. Even the glow of the computer screen is visible.

"Do you want to talk?" I ask her and her only response is that her fingers stop moving across the keys.

She doesn't turn to face me or give any sign that I've spoken to her.

"I don't want to fight, Kat," I tell her and force every bit of emotion into my words. "I don't want this."

She turns slowly in her seat, a baggy t-shirt covering her body to her upper thighs. Her exposed skin is pale and the dark room makes her look that much paler. Her green eyes give her away though. Nothing but sadness there.

My body is pulled to her, and I can't help it. I can't stand that look in her eyes. Before I can tell her I love her and I'm sorry, before I can come up with some lame excuse, she cuts me off.

"I wanted to last night," she says and then crosses her arms. She looks uncomfortable and unnatural. Like she's doing what she thinks she should be doing.

"I'm here now," I tell her and walk closer to her. There's a set of chairs in the corner of the room from our first apartment and I almost drag one over, but I'm too afraid to break eye contact with her.

At least she's looking at me, talking to me, receptive to what I have to say.

"Ask me whatever you want," I tell her and deep down I'm screaming. Because I know I'll answer her. I'll tell her everything just to take that pain away, even if it's only temporary, even if it fucks her too.

Her doe eyes widen slightly and she cowers back, swallowing before answering me. "Aren't you tired?" she says softly and her eyes flicker to the door and then to the floor.

She doesn't want to know the truth.

"Yeah, I'm exhausted. But I'm not going to bed until you do." I lick my lips and clear my throat, hoping she'll give in to me. For weeks I tried to stay up with her or brush off the fact that I'd pass out while she was still working and vice versa.

"I can stay up for you," I offer her. It's not what she wants, but it's something.

"Well this has to get done, and it's going to take hours."

"I can wait," I tell her but the second the words slip out she turns back to the computer and says, "Don't."

With her back to me and her fingers already flying across the keys again, I've never felt more alone and dejected.

"I'll go unpack and relax on the bed then," I tell her, gripping the door to stay upright and keep myself from ripping her out of that chair and bringing her to bed.

She whips around in the chair and asks, “Here?”

It takes me a moment to realize why the hell she’s asking me that and when I do, it’s like a bullet to the chest.

A mix of emotions swell in my gut and heat my blood. Anger is there, but the dejectedness is what cuts me the most.

“Is that alright?” I ask sarcastically.

She nods, conceding to let me stay in my own damn house, but the look in her eyes doesn’t fade. She really wants me out. She wants me to just leave? Did she think I wouldn’t fight for her? That I’d let this destroy us? It may ruin me, but I’ll be damned if I let it ruin *us*.

“I said I don’t want a divorce.” My words come out hard. I’m sick of this. “I want you,” I tell her with conviction and walk closer to her, not leaving any space between us.

“I don’t know what I want,” Kat says, gripping the armrests of the desk chair as her lips turn down into a painful frown and her eyes gloss over. Like she’s on the verge of breaking. The last thread she was holding has snapped, leaving her falling. I’m not there to catch her, because I’m the one that pushed her over the edge. And I hate myself for it.

It's my fault, and this is all on me, but I'll make it right.

"You don't have to, Kat," I tell her and move just a little closer. I need a chance. She's vulnerable; I can feel it coming off of her in waves.

I cup her cheek in my hand to lean down and kiss her, but she pushes back, quickly standing and making the desk chair slam against the desk.

My pride, my ego, whatever it is that makes a man is destroyed in this moment. My limbs freeze and the tension makes me feel like I'm breaking. Literally cracking in my very center.

I lick my lips, finally letting out a breath as Kat whispers, "I'm sorry, I'm just ..."

She doesn't finish, and I have to look up at her before I can stand upright again.

"You just what?" I ask her.

"I don't know, Evan," she says with desperation in her voice.

"Don't think," I tell her, grasping for anything to keep her from running. "Just let me make it better," I offer and she stands there, in nothing but that t-shirt and looks at me as if I'm both her savior and her enemy.

I walk slow, each step making the floor creak ever so

quietly. I don't rush it until I'm close enough to her to feel her heat. And she lets me, standing still and giving me the chance I need.

My lips crash against hers, my body pressing against hers and forcing her back. Each step she takes, I take one with her.

"Stop," she tells me and pushes me away. My breathing is ragged as my hands clench to keep from holding on to her as she leaves me. I can still taste her, my body ringing with desire to make it up to her.

To ease her pain and remind her how good I make her feel. It's what she needs. It's been weeks and I can't deny I need her even more. I need to bury myself inside her heat.

My fingers wrap around her hips and I push her back against the wall. Her arms wrap around my neck and she comes in for the kiss this time. Taking the passion from me, letting me give her what she needs. The comfort and escape from reality. A welcome distraction to the fact that our marriage is at risk.

In this moment there's nothing but what we feel for each other. Nothing else. No logic or reason. Just the devotion and intense desire.

I'm grateful it still exists. I only wish this moment would

last forever. Where we're both weak for each other, desperate and drunk with lust.

"You're mine, Kat," I whisper in her ear. My breath is hot and it's making the air between us that much hotter.

Her back arches against the wall and she pushes her soft body into mine. A quiet moan spills from her sweet lips. I stare at her face, the expression of utter rapture with her eyes closed and her lips parted just slightly.

I rock my palm over and over, putting pressure on her swollen nub and feeling her cunt get hotter and wetter.

"This is mine," I whisper louder, not holding back the possession in my voice.

A strangled groan fills the air. At first I don't know if it's from me or her, but the sweet cadence of her voice prolongs the sound of pleasure as her body writhes against mine. She's so close.

I tear the thin lace fabric of her panties off in one tug and watch her face as her eyes pop open. The gorgeous green stares back at me with a mix of emotions, the overwhelming two being desire and vulnerability.

I don't give her the chance to second-guess this. This is how we're meant to be. Together, raw and bared.

I only release my grip on her to unzip my pants. The sound mixes with Kat's heavy breathing.

"Evan," she whispers my name as if it's a question.

She wants me, although she knows we shouldn't do this. Fuck, I know she's going to question this. Maybe even regret it. But she just needs to feel me again; she needs this as much as I do.

I press the head of my dick against her opening, and slide myself through her slick folds, teasing her and watching as her eyes close tight and she squirms when I just barely touch her clit.

So close.

"Evan," she whispers and this time it's a plea. One I can satisfy.

In one swift stroke I slam into her, buried deep and making her scream out.

Her nails dig into my shoulders as her body's forced against the wall and her head falls back.

I kiss her throat ravenously, desperate to taste her, but not willing to mute the sounds of pleasure she's making.

My thrusts are primal, ruthless. I take from her over and over. Each time her back hits the wall and her whimpers get louder and louder.

Her grip gets tighter as my balls draw up. My spine tingles with the need to cum, but I need her to cum with me. I'm desperate to feel her walls tighten around my dick. Desperate to feel her pulsing and milking me for my cum.

And the moment I think I can't take anymore, she gives me what I need. Screaming out my name as her orgasm rips through her body.

"Fuck," I groan into the crook of her neck. My dick pulses and I cum hard, buried deep inside of her pussy. My heart hammers hard and fast and refuses to stop as she clings to me for dear life. Her eyes are closed and her teeth are digging into her bottom lip when I finally look at her.

"I love you, Kat," I whisper as I pull away from her, finally breathing and starting to come down from the highest high.

"I love …" Kat starts to reply, but she doesn't finish. She doesn't look me in the eyes.

She's so ashamed to love me, she can't even say it back.

CHAPTER 9

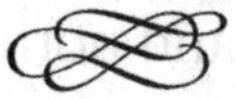

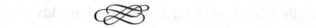

Kat

So weak and pathetic, I don't deserve to heal.
The deceit I've accepted is all that lets me feel.
Hold back the lies, let truth die, I accept the painful pill.
Just hold me tight, I won't fight. Yours to keep, and yours to kill.

I don't know what I'm more ashamed about as I toss the throw blanket over the sofa and make myself get up.

The fact that I fucked my husband.

Or the fact that I then refused to go to bed with him.

Not that I told him that. I hid behind work and then snuck out here, to the living room. I didn't sleep on the sofa for more than a few hours. Maybe that's what I deserve for being so weak and falling right into his arms the moment he pulled me in.

It's like a spiraling dark hole and I'm falling deeper and deeper, to the point where what I want and what I'm feeling don't make sense and nothing adds up.

I couldn't possibly feel more pathetic at this point. And it's because of him.

Because I love him and hate myself for it.

I glance at my phone on the dining room table as I make my way to the kitchen. I already know what Sue would say. She'd feel sorry for me for going back to the man who cheated on me.

Pity and sorrow for the pathetic girl, clinging to an unfaithful man. Even the bitter thought echoes what part of me feels.

The thing about love though is that it's not a light switch. You can't just turn it off. You can't erase the memories and move on. She knows that much, she just chooses to forget it.

My head throbs and I'm not sure if it's from the lack of sleep or caffeine. Even the faint sounds of city life from stories down are enough to make my temples pulse.

I groan as I rest against the wall of the living room and try to calm the headache. I close my eyes and feel the weight of all the stress from the last two weeks.

I need aspirin or coffee. Or both. My heart sputters as I slowly walk up the stairs, knowing Evan's lying in bed alone and that it was my choice.

As I pass the office I remember last night and my thighs clench; I can still feel him inside of me. I can feel his lips on my neck, his rough hands on my body. Taking from me. Relentlessly, possessively. Each step brings my body temperature higher and higher, yet my heart hurts more and more.

Why won't the pain just go away? Why can't my head just shut the fuck up so I can pretend I'm okay for just a moment?

The bedroom door is open and as I walk through the door, I can't take my eyes off the perfectly made bed. The cream and white comforter with black dahlias is pulled tight, looking pristine. A crease forms in the center of my forehead as I walk to the bathroom, listening to my heart beat with each step, but finding the bathroom empty. *Evan wasn't downstairs,* I think as I open the cabinet and silently grab the bottle of aspirin. He wasn't downstairs, and he's not up here.

I swallow the pills without water, staring into the mirror

as my heart clenches. Did he even stay last night? Did he find me asleep on the sofa and decide to leave? *It's what I wanted, wasn't it?*

The cabinet door slams shut; I give the push more force than I meant to, but I ignore it, walking quickly down to the kitchen.

I just need coffee. Coffee will wake me, rid me of this headache and give me the energy I need to deal with this mess.

And it's such a chaotic mess. A mix of emotions and desires that thrashes me side to side like an unforgiving earthquake. The only thing certain is that I can't stand on my own two feet. At least not without a cup of coffee.

A sarcastic huff of a laugh leaves me as I round the bottom of the stairs and head to the kitchen, a pitiful smile adorning my lips.

I suppose I can live a sad and pathetic life. Maybe I'll be a cat lady, a woman who works herself into the ground. I've never thought much of what I would be.

Using the cup next to the sink, I fill the glass with water and pour it into the back of the coffee maker, remembering the days when having a child was on my mind. Back when my career was a dream, when my time was monopolized by Evan and we owned the world together. We could be and do anything we wanted.

I slip the K-Cup into the machine and turn it on as I remember how he'd hold my belly and plant a kiss there, just below my belly button, telling me what a wonderful mother I would be one day to his son.

We were fools. I knew this would never last. I knew it back then. Just like I know it now.

I lick my lips and take in a heavy breath, slipping the ceramic mug with *Rise and Shine* scrolled on the side under the spigot to the coffee machine.

I would say that was back when I was young and stupid, but I still am young and stupid, aren't I?

My bare feet pad on the tiled kitchen floor as I open the fridge and search for the coffee creamer. I stare longer than I should at the empty spot on the shelf. I can't even remember to get creamer. My teeth grind back and forth and the throb comes back with a vengeance in my temples.

I slam the fridge door shut as the coffee maker sputters to life. It's quite something when you've fallen so hard that a mundane task like going to the grocery store is enough to push you over the edge. Maybe I've truly gone crazy.

The front door opening is the last thing I need right now.

The door closes softly, like Evan didn't want to wake me. I wipe under my eyes and push my hair out of my face as I lean against the wall with my arms crossed, waiting for him to make his way in here.

I can't explain why I feel guilty. It's all I feel. Is this normal? I feel like this is what I deserve. Like somehow I've orchestrated all of this just so I could feel lonely and miserable. Maybe I just had it too good and I decided I needed to go right back to the mental space I used to drown in.

"Morning." I hear Evan's voice and the sound of a plastic bag crinkling before I see him.

My lips part to tell him good morning, but then I catch sight of him.

He looks tired, his scruff a little too grown out, his dark hair a little too long and a bit of darkness under his eyes. For the first time I've laid eyes on him, he looks older, more mature but still as handsome as ever.

His jaw tenses as he rests the bag on the counter and then looks over his shoulder at me. "Did you sleep well?" he asks me, barely looking at me before turning his attention to the corner cabinet and grabbing a mug for himself.

"No," I force the word out. "Evan," I try to talk but my

heart slams at the same time that Evan shuts the cabinet and turns around to face me. He leaves the stark white mug on the granite countertop and I stare at it, rather than at him.

I have to spend time away from him. That's what I really need. To get used to being alone again.

"I need you to leave," I tell Evan and then peek up at him. It hurts to say the words after last night. I should have said them before, but I was so tired and felt so alone. I just needed him then. I used him in a way, but I won't do it again. I won't keep pretending.

He shakes his head, not once or twice but continuously as if he's in disbelief. Like I didn't actually tell him that. He had to know it was going to come to this.

"Last night," he starts to say and I cut him off.

"Was a mistake," I tell him forcefully and my voice cracks. My chest feels tight and it's harder to breathe, but I stand my ground.

"We're different people, Evan." I try to talk but my words are stuck in my throat.

"We've always been different, Kat. Always," Evan says and his words come out hard. I can already hear him convincing me. I can already see myself falling right back into his arms because that's where I feel so safe and so loved. But he can't hold me forever.

"I can't do this, Evan," I tell him honestly, feeling my heart break. It's a slow break, one meant to be torturous.

"Do what?" he asks me cautiously and it pisses me off. The plastic bag crinkles as he reaches behind him, brushing against it and bracing himself against the counter.

"This. I can't." I look him in the eyes even as mine water. I let the tears fall as my blood turns to ice, yet my skin heats.

Evan takes a step toward me, my name falling from his lips and his arms open.

"Get out!" I yell at him, feeling the weakness threatening to consume me. Threatening to bring me right back to him. "I don't want this. I don't want you here."

"It's going to be alright," he tries to tell me, that placating tone in his voice making me even angrier.

"Well it's not now, and you need to get the fuck out," I seethe. My body trembles as I look him in the eyes and tell him again. "I need space, and that means you leaving." This townhouse is in both our names, I'm more than aware of that and he could easily bring that up. He has a right to be here and part of me wishes he would, but he doesn't. He stares at the ground for a moment, his broad shoulders rising slowly with each heavy breath. My body shakes as he snatches his keys off the counter and leaves, slamming the door behind him.

I try to convince myself as I move to the counter, bracing my hot palms on the cold stone and focusing on breathing. This is the worst it's ever been between us. And I know it's the end of us. I can feel it deep down in my bones. Shattering my core.

Out of the need to move, to do something and just go through the motions, I reach for the bag on the counter.

It's a mistake. Inside is a bottle of coffee creamer.

It's so stupid that something like this could shred me. That it can make me fall to the floor. That it can make me feel like I've made the worst decision of my life.

That it makes me feel like I'm alone. And that it's my fault for pushing Evan away.

CHAPTER 10

Evan

It happened so slowly,
So slowly I couldn't see.
She ruined me, damned me,
And brought me to my knees.
I can't deny there was only one,
Only her for me.
One true love is a lie,
But with her, it has to be.

It's funny how love was there right from the start and I didn't even know it.

Looking around my old bedroom in my father's house reminds me of all the times I spent here, but more than anything the last time I was in here. When I was crying like a bitch on my bed, burying my head into the pillow and refusing to accept that my mother was dying.

I glance at it, the red plaid flannel sheets tucked in tight. Kat did that. She made the bed the next morning. She held me all night. She let me cry and didn't tell me to stop. She just loved me.

I think she loved me from the very beginning though.

I remember that first date we had a few days after meeting her. I could still feel the beat of the heavy music in the club pumping through my veins as I opened the door to my apartment on the edge of Brooklyn. I looked over my shoulder to take a peek at her, knowing the alcohol was wearing off and what I wanted was more than obvious.

I could tell she was surprised by how nice my place was. There's a lot of remodeling going on in the city and I spent my money wisely, always have.

The second the door closed, my hands were all over her just like they had been in the taxi and in the club. We were magnetized toward each other.

That's why I think it was love. Lust is one thing. It comes and goes. And the moment you're filled and satisfied, disinterest takes its place. But that's never been the case for us. There was always more. Even as we grew apart, it only made what could be that much more tempting.

I turn the lights off in my bedroom as a distant siren drowns the silence of the room and headlights from a passing car leave stripes of light moving through the small room.

Again, I remember what we used to have. Who we used to be. The first night is all I can think about. The day she ruined me forever. And I didn't even know it was happening.

She wrapped that sweet mouth of hers around my dick before I could stop her. We'd only just gotten inside and I was planning on moving a little slower. I would've skipped the foreplay and gone straight for what I wanted. I wasn't going to tell her no though.

I was paralyzed as she dug her fingers into my thighs and sucked her way down my length. Her cheeks hollowed as she moaned and I swear I almost came just from the sight of her.

My balls tightened as she pulled back, letting my dick pop out of her mouth and then licking the tip. Her tongue slid up my slit as she worked my shaft and then did it again. The sight of her on her knees and practically worshipping my dick is something I can never forget. It was the shock mostly, I think. A woman who was already too good for me. A woman who was probably slumming it, was on her knees devouring me and loving every second of it.

My fingers speared through her hair as I closed my eyes and let myself enjoy it. Only for a moment though. I wanted more of her and I was sure I only had the night.

Time moved so slowly as I savored each second of her, wanting more and knowing I could have it, but not ready for it to end.

She stared up at me, licking her lips and shaking her head when I tugged on her to come up and stop. Her lips were already swollen as she panted and then leaned forward. Ignoring me and taking what she wanted.

I watched as she closed her eyes and pushed me all the way to the back of her throat, forcing me to groan from deep in my chest. I fisted my hand in her hair and pulled her off of me; it was fucking torture, wanting what she was giving me, but knowing I'd need more.

"Strip down," I groaned out, my head leaned back and my eyes closed. As if I had any control at all over her.

She shook her head again and I couldn't believe the plea that slipped from her lips.

"I want you to cum in my mouth." She said it so simply, but full of truth. Her voice was laced with desire, but it was the way her shoulders rose and fell with her heavy breathing and the way she scooted closer to me, eager and begging for more that convinced me.

I could never say no to Kat. She doesn't ask for a damn thing. Never has, and I've wished she would. I'd give her the world if I could. But that night there was no fucking way I was going to deny her that.

I'm a selfish man, after all.

I slipped my hand around the back of her head as my toes curled. I was almost embarrassed by how quickly she made me come.

She didn't stop swallowing until I was spent and even then, she bobbed lightly on my dick and sucked like she wanted more. My greedy little sex kitten.

After she was done with me, when I'd pulled my pants up and stared down at her, the atmosphere changed.

"I don't have sex on the first date," she said shyly, a blush rising to her cheeks as she slowly stood up, trying to keep her balance by gripping onto my arm. She was hesitant, embarrassed maybe. I think it was vulnerability. I think she was afraid I'd be done. *She was afraid it was only lust.*

"Oh yeah," I responded, still trying to catch my breath and get a sense of who this girl was. "So what's this then?"

When I looked in her eyes, I knew what the real reason was. She thought I'd be done with her if I got her in bed.

More importantly, it meant she wanted to keep me.

The pride that filled my chest at the thought has never felt so good.

She wanted more and all the same, she was terrified to have me. Maybe scared she couldn't keep me, or scared to keep me. I still can't tell which was the motivating factor.

The thought made my still-hard dick even harder. And I stroked myself once and then again until she noticed. A smirk lifted up my lips as I saw her eyes widen.

"What if I want you? What if I want to take care of you now?" I asked her, taking a step forward and forcing her backward. Her knees hit the bed and she nearly collapsed, the heat growing between us and nearly suffocating me.

I kissed my way down her neck, letting the heat between us get higher and higher.

"Not just yet," I said as I stroked my dick again, feeling it turn hard as steel again already. "Let me taste you," I whispered.

Her gorgeous eyes peeked up at me through her thick lashes.

"Take it easy on me, will ya?" she asked me, again feigning a strength that wasn't quite there. She was vulnerable and weak for me. Both of us knew it, only she was pretending she wasn't.

It's something that made me crave her more.

"Sure," I whispered in her ear as I pushed her onto the bed. But I never had any intention of holding back when it came to her.

I fucked her as hard as I could into that mattress. I buried myself inside her and held off as long as I could, taking her higher and higher each time until she was holding on to me for her life. Her nails scratched and dug into my skin as she screamed out my name.

I destroyed her the best way I could. And I've never been more proud of anything else in my life.

She's an emotional woman, Kat is. I didn't see it at first, but that night, our first night, I knew it. I could practically hear her tell me she loved me. If nothing else, I know she loved what I did to her.

I wanted to hear her tell me those words so badly. More than anything else, I wanted *this* woman to admit it. She fell in love with me that first night.

I was desperate for it.

I didn't realize that night that the look in her eyes was exactly what I felt too. Desperate to keep her, but knowing it was never supposed to happen.

I whip around, facing the door as the sound of someone coming brings me back to today. Six years later, that night is just a distant memory.

The door to my bedroom opens wide, creaking as it does and revealing my father. I haven't seen him like this in a long damn time.

His hair's been gray for a while, but it's just a bit too long and in a t-shirt and flannel pants, he looks older. Beaten down even. Just a few years can change everything. Has it been that long since I really looked at him?

"You getting comfortable in here?" Pops asks me as he walks in and takes a look at the dresser. He runs his hand along it and then makes a face as he turns his hand over and sees the dust there. As he wipes off his hand on the flannel pajamas he adds, "It's about time you came back to clean your room."

A rough chuckle barely makes its way up my chest.

"When are you moving out of this place?" I ask him, jokingly.

"When I'm dead and gone," my father answers me the same way he has for years now. Ever since Ma left, I've wanted him to move. He won't though and I can't blame him.

"Good thing I'm not in a nursing home. Don't think you'd like to crash there, would you?"

I give him a tight smile, feeling nothing but shame. I lick my bottom lip and run my hand through my hair searching for some sort of an explanation, but I can't lie to my father and I don't want to tell him the truth.

"I messed up before with your mother, you know. She kicked me out. I thought it was over." My father flicks on the light and walks toward the bed, ignoring the fact that I just wanted to pass out and try to sleep.

"I was younger than you though. By the time I was your age, we'd had you. I'd settled down and stopped being stupid."

"What'd you do?" I ask my father out of genuine curiosity. I'd never seen anything but love from my parents. They never fought in front of me and the one time I came home early, catching them in the heat of a fight, they stopped immediately.

Later that night, when I was sitting in front of the TV, cross-legged and way too close, all I could hear was him apologizing in the kitchen. It'd been quiet all afternoon and night.

"I don't want you to go to bed mad at me," I heard him tell her.

It was the only fight I'd ever witnessed and I remember being scared that he'd done something that Ma wasn't going to forgive.

But she did. I never asked back then, and I'm sure if I did he wouldn't remember. And this fight he's talking about obviously isn't that.

"What do you think?" he answers me. "We were young and stupid and had a bad fight over money or something. I got drunk, kissed a girl at a bar. I felt like shit about it and she smacked me right across the face too." He smirks at the memory. "She beat the hell out of me. Kicked me out." The smile falls and he shakes his head as he adds, "I deserved it."

"I can't imagine you ever doing that."

"I loved your mother. I was angry at her over something stupid, I can't even remember what."

The silence stretches between us as he struggles to come up with what to say next. "I proposed to her a few months after we got back together." A huff of a laugh leaves him and he adds, "God rest her soul," as he twists the wedding band around his ring finger. He's never taken it off. For the same reason he'll never leave this house.

He still needs her. Even if it's just the memory of her.

"The point is, we all make mistakes," he says and then squares his shoulders at me, raising both of his hands and shaking them, "when we're young and allowed to be stupid."

"I'm not that old," I tell him halfheartedly. I know what he's getting at, but I don't need to be lectured. I'm well aware of how stupid I've been. He's the one who has no idea how badly I've fucked up.

The silence stretches between us and all I can think about is every position I've put myself in where not being faithful to my wife would have been easier than it should be. I focus on that and not the night that still haunts me.

"What are you doing, Evan?" my father asks as I dump my bag on the bed. "You've fucked up more than you should have. You're too old to be carrying on like this."

My initial reaction is to bite back that he's wrong. That he has no idea what's going on. But it wouldn't matter.

I nod my head and let the strap from the bag fall off my shoulder. "Yeah, I know, Pops."

"You need to make this right," he tells me, holding my gaze and pointing a finger at me.

I swallow thickly, knowing he's right. But I haven't got a clue how to make this better. I can't take back what's been done.

I'm fucked.

CHAPTER 11

Kat

Just get it over with,
Tell me that we're done.
Leave me to this madness,
I accept that you have won.

You've broken me to pieces,
Left me numb and blind.
Made me only yours-
I've completely lost my mind.

"I need a distraction, that's what I need," I speak the words on my mind without really thinking about it. We've been here in Jules' house helping her unpack for at least two hours now, and everyone's been kind enough to not only *not* ask about what's going on, but to not treat me like I'm some wounded animal either. I'm grateful, but I need to talk. I need to just let it all out and have someone sift through this mess and give me a straight answer as to what I should do.

I roll my eyes at the internal thought. I'm a grown woman. I should know what to do and make the decision with certainty. But I've never felt so uncertain in my life.

"That makes sense," Maddie says and nods her head as she takes out a picture frame, wrapped in thick brown packing paper. She's careful with it as she removes the paper and exposes the silver frame. "Distractions are a good thing," she says with a small nod. "Sometimes," she adds.

I don't know what's in it, but whatever it is, it makes her smile.

"I can't go home to the townhouse with all his shit there and lie in the bed that we've had together for forever." I purge the thought from me, feeling lighter and lighter with each word. "I can't hide in my office and do the same shit over and over again."

I stare at the artwork centered over Julia's fireplace as I talk. I don't really care what anyone else thinks; I need a break from this, some kind of getaway.

The crinkling of the packaging paper is all I can hear from the other side of the expansive room. It's so loud that I'm not sure anyone but Maddie even heard me. We've been working in relative silence save for the soft sound of music flowing from the kitchen behind us.

"We should go on a girls' trip," I offer up and look over my shoulder at Maddie. I shift in my seat and wait for her to look back at me.

"Hell yeah," she answers without hesitation.

"What does the newlywed think?" Maddie asks Jules and instantly Jules brightens.

She shrugs, as if the word *newlywed* didn't make her day and puts the attention back on me as she says, "I'm happy to do whatever you want, Kat." Jules is holding back, and I can tell. I think it's because she's happy. Her life is renewed and she's filled with nothing but happiness. And here I am, falling apart and stealing from her joy.

"You're glowing," I tell her and wait for a response, feeling guilty. My chest feels tight and I shift into a cross-legged position on the plush carpet and grab the plastic bottle of water, drinking it down slowly even though it's room temperature now.

Maddie quirks an eyebrow. "You already make a baby?" she asks.

“Shut up,” Jules says playfully and then goes to the granite counter behind us and makes a show of drinking from her glass of wine. We exchange amused looks, waiting for her to reply.

“Not yet,” Jules finally answers.

“Yet!” Maddie practically shrieks. “First comes love, then comes marriage-”

“Then comes a new home and a fresh start,” Jules cuts her off and Sue laughs from her spot in the corner of the living room.

It’s grand and spacious and much more like Jules’ style. She got a deal on this home and the amount of space is making me regret buying a place so close to the park. It reminds me how tiny our townhouse is. At least compared to this.

But this is a family home, and I live in a townhouse that’s not meant for anything more than two people. I force my lips to stay in place and swallow down the frown and all the feelings threatening to come up.

I made this decision. I need to own up to it and deal with the consequences.

“I’m not sure I can do this girls’ trip,” Sue says and then chews the inside of her cheek. She braces herself on the chair before rising and picking up her wine glass. “I’ve got a new boss and he's a dick with a capital D. There's no way he's going to give me time off."

"It's not really his position to give it to you," Maddie says skeptically. "Like you *earn* your days. And we haven't even set a date yet." The defensiveness in Maddie's voice catches me off guard.

Sue walks closer to us, a glass of wine in her right hand and a ball of packaging paper in her left. "He'll give me shit." She shrugs like it's no big deal, but Maddie isn't having it.

"So fuck him," Maddie says, a little anger coming out. She doesn't usually get worked up, so I'm taken aback.

"It's fine, it was just a thought," I offer up and try to smooth the tension flowing between the two of them.

"You okay?" I ask her and Maddie ignores me, picking up her wine glass filled with pinot grigio and throwing it back.

"I don't want to set a bad precedent," Sue says staring directly at Maddie, who refuses to look back at Suzette.

My gaze moves between the two of them and I'm only distracted by the loud clap behind me from Jules. "Who wants some cheese?" she says behind me and we all turn slowly to see her lifting a tray of cut meats and cheese as if it's the peace treaty between us.

Sue has the decency to laugh and the small moment of tension is immediately relieved.

I feel odd sitting in this room and unpacking all of Jules' odds and ends. Looking around the room, I'm surrounded by friends, but I feel alone. I take another sip of water. It's all in my head, I'm more than aware of that, but it doesn't change how I feel.

Jules has a new life with a fresh start, but she's afraid to be happy about it. Maybe that's only because I'm here. She doesn't want her new marriage to cause me any more pain. She's sweet like that, but it only makes it hurt worse.

"Have you slept with him?" Jules asks me as she grabs a contraption from one of her drawers that she uses to uncork the wine bottles. The kitchen is all white. White cabinets and a sleek white countertop. The only color is in the ebony floorboards.

"Who with who?" Maddie asks with a sly smile on her face. "Is Sue sleeping with her boss?" Her question makes Suzette tense and stare back at Maddie with daggers. But Maddie's oblivious.

"Kat," Jules says and her tone is casual, not sympathetic or pushy, no motive apparent. "Have you slept with Evan since it all happened?" she asks and pops the cork from the bottle, keeping her attention on it rather than on me.

My face heats, knowing the other two women are looking at me, but I wait for Jules. The second she raises her eyes to mine, although it was only meant to be a glance, I nod my head.

I anticipate the scoff of disdain from Sue, the tilted head with a sympathetic look from Maddie, but I don't know what to expect from Jules.

She shrugs her shoulders, the cream chenille sweater slipping down and making her look that much thinner, that much more beautiful. "Was it any good?" she asks and lifts the glass to her lips. It's dark red wine, the same color she wears on her lips. It's one thing I like about Jules; she's nothing if not consistent. But this is new territory for us to be in.

I roll my eyes and then wipe my face with my hand. It's always good with Evan. "It was a mistake," I answer her instead.

"People make mistakes," Jules says low, so low I almost didn't hear her. And then she looks at me and adds, "It's okay. I get it." She sounds so sad and I can't help but to wonder what's going on with her. For just a moment, a short glimpse, there's something there other than the perfect façade she always carries. But the moment she registers that I can see it, the crack in her demeanor, she straightens her shoulders and takes in a heavy breath.

Silence passes and the only thing that can be heard is the rustling of paper as Maddie wraps something up. I've never felt so alone and unwelcomed. But it's not them, it's me and my head, I know it is. "I just don't know what to do," I tell her, biting back the questions on the tip of my tongue.

"You don't need to decide right now," Jules says easily. "There's a lot to consider and talk about." She nods her head as she talks, almost like she's talking to herself.

"The thing is," I hesitate, although being around Jules makes me feel centered. She's not going to judge me, but the other two women … I can feel it already and I can't say that I blame them.

"I don't know what I want, but I know he'll convince me to stay with him."

"Men have a way with words," Sue says and drains her glass before standing up and smoothing out her pants. "It's called lying."

I bite my tongue as I tilt my head to watch Sue walk to the kitchen. She's taking bites of the cheese board and then glancing at the piles of boxes still lining the wall of the kitchen.

"I mean some men," Sue says softly and then clears her throat to add with a touch of sympathy, "I keep letting my shitty experience color my opinion. "Sorry," she says looking me in the eyes.

"Thanks," I tell her but in all honesty, she's not wrong.

"So you're indecisive, and that makes sense. You're married. You love him. But you're hurt." Maddie talks like it's so simple and easy to comprehend. But it's not. There's a raging war of emotions inside of me. I don't know that I can trust my husband, and that alone is enough to end it and what pushed me to kick him out this morning.

Rather than confess about my lack of trust, I offer a partial truth.

"I slept with him last night and then kicked him out this morning." I shake my head realizing how awful that sounds, how crazy it seems.

"Sounds like a divorce to me," Sue says and then fills her glass again. "I did it for years, Kat. Years of back and forth. Forgiving but not forgetting." Her slender fingers play on the stem of the glass. "Wish I had those years back."

I feel desperate for her to understand. I get that her marriage failed and I see the similarities. But this is different, isn't it? I'm not ready for this to end. As pathetic as it sounds, I already feel alone again and I don't want that. I want the love I had with Evan. I just want it back.

"I don't know what I did that pushed him away." Even as I say the words, I know that's not true. I let distance grow between us. I ignored him in favor of my career.

"Nothing, it's not you. It's not your fault." Sue's words are hard, with no negotiation allowed. So I don't correct her.

"Why are you with someone you don't trust?" she asks me, a bit of aggression in her voice.

"I just wanted him last night," I say and my voice is soft and I feel myself slipping, falling into that pathetic black hole where all I do is blame myself.

Sue's eyes are soft as is her voice when she asks, "Do you want to be together, or no?" she asks me.

Before I can tell her how messed up my head is right now, Maddie says, "It's whatever she wants. They can be friends with benefits if that's what she wants, fuck buddies, she can use him for revenge sex. Who cares? It's none of your business and pushing her to decide is bullshit."

We all sit stunned for a moment; Maddie looks out of breath as she picks at the paper in her hands. She doesn't look up.

"I'll figure it out," I spit out the words. Everyone in the room looks as uneasy as I feel and I regret coming here. I regret trying to move forward without knowing where I'm going.

Sue leaves the room and I stare at the fireplace mantel as the bathroom door opens and closes and then Maddie gets up to follow Sue.

I regret last night and this morning.

I regret trying to explain my mess of emotions and poor decisions.

I regret everything and I don't know what to do right now, or even tomorrow that I know with certainty I won't regret immediately after.

CHAPTER 12

EVAN

I refuse to leave,
Refuse to tell her goodbye.
I'll be with her for always,
Until the day I die.
It's selfish, and I hate myself,
But she's the only one.
Who makes this life worth living-
Who makes me come undone.

I tried it. I swear I tried to give her space.

She says that's what she needs, but I know it's not. She needs me. Period. She needs me to be there and that's where I've failed. Not just in the last few weeks. I chose a lifestyle that forced us apart.

I can fix this, but not by running to Pops and leaving her all alone with nothing but this city whispering in her ear.

My arm stiffens as I slide the key into the lock. My heart doesn't beat until it turns, proving she didn't change the locks. I let out a breath I didn't know I was still holding and push it open. I'm prepared with what I need to say. Prepared to hold my ground and not take no for an answer.

But it only takes one step inside of our living room for all of it to slip away from me.

Kat looks so tired, so worn out propped up in the corner of the sofa with her laptop sitting to the left of her, but the screen's black. She has a cup of coffee in her hands although she has bags under her eyes. She turns to me slowly, wiping the sleep from her eyes and adjusting herself slightly.

"What are you doing here?" she asks me, still seated with her legs tucked underneath her on the sofa. I'm stunned for a moment, because she's so fucking beautiful, even in this state. My body's drawn to her. And if it were another time, I'd go to the sofa, push the laptop off and lie down, taking her into my arms.

And she'd let me.

"This is my house." I try not to say the words too firmly.

"Our house," I correct myself and swallow before continuing and taking a single step closer to her. "I worked my ass off-"

"Then I'll move out," Kat quickly states matter-of-factly, but the pain is barely disguised. She seems to snap out of whatever daze had her captive before I came in here.

"I don't want you to move out. We don't need this." I emphasize my words.

"I asked for time and space because I don't know what to do, Evan. You aren't giving me any options without telling me what happened."

"You want to know?" I look her in the eyes, feeling my blood pulse harder in my veins.

"Are you going to tell me the truth?" she asks me in a cracked whisper. "All of it?"

All of it? I have to break her gaze. I can't. I can't confess everything. I'd lose her forever.

The second I break eye contact, she scoffs. "You're so full of shit. Why are you doing this to me?" she asks me, although it's rhetorical.

"I just want to be home with you while this blows over."

"Blows over?" she practically yells. I'm not good with

words. I never have been, but I wish I had the wisdom to say the right thing right now.

“Maybe this is the moment,” she says while rolling her eyes with a sad smile on her beautiful face.

“The moment?” I dare to ask.

“The moment that changes everything for the rest of my life. I’ve been wondering exactly what moment it was, but maybe it hasn’t happened yet.”

Her words settle deep in my very core. Slow, yet all-consuming. Her face changes from the sarcastic disappointment that she had when she said the words. As if only just now realizing the magnitude of them herself.

“We can go back,” I tell her softly, raising my hands just slightly, but the fear of losing her keeps my blood cold and my motions subtle.

“It’s called separating for a reason,” she tells me. As if what we had the other night meant nothing. As if there’s no reason for us to be together. Maybe she really doesn’t love me anymore.

“We didn’t decide to do that,” I answer her. “You were angry.”

“Rightfully so,” she spits back.

“I told you it’s not true,” I tell her as I stare deep into her eyes. I watch as they gloss over and her lower lip trembles. "Just …" I swallow thickly, the lump growing in the back of my throat suffocating any plea I have for her. *Just love me. Just forgive me.*

I lick my lips and turn away from her, not able to voice what I'm feeling. I slowly take a seat in the side chair, and it creaks as I rest my weight in it. Kat starts to get up.

"I don't want to fight," I tell her.

"I don't want this, Evan. I didn't ask for this," she raises her voice, the anger coming back. She doesn't move though, and I can tell she's losing the fight.

"I don't know what to do or say, or what to think. I feel crazy!" She stares at me wide-eyed. "Do you understand what that's like? To be so fucking stupid? To know I'm being stupid and setting myself up for you to hurt me."

"I won't hurt you-"

"But you did! And you won't even tell me why." Her shoulders shudder, but she doesn't cry, she holds her ground.

"I don't want to lose you, Kat," I manage to speak and peek up to look at her.

"I want you to quit," she says and rocks on her feet. She nods her head and visibly swallows. "You need to quit."

She stares at me, her eyes pleading. Her body's still, like she's not breathing.

"It's not that easy," I tell her and God I wish she knew. I want to tell her everything, but I can't risk it. I can't leave right now. I just need time.

"It is that easy; you quit or leave." I stare into her eyes that swirl with nothing but raw vulnerability, and hesitate.

"You're going to give me an ultimatum?" But even as I ask her, I know that's what she's doing.

She has no idea.

I just need time. I need her to just give me time. As soon as I'm out of this, I can do whatever she wants.

But not right now.

I can feel her slipping away. Every second that passes that I don't tell her, she's turning colder toward me. But she can't know. No one can.

My lips part and I can feel my lungs still. The words are right there. Begging me, and desperate for her to hear. I need her more than anything.

"Kat," I say her name but it's so much more. It's me begging for her to love me blindly, to trust that I love her and that I'd never do anything to hurt her.

I can't. I can't risk her, and I won't do it.

My mouth closes and I turn away from her, running my hand over my face.

"Get out," Kat says and her voice hitches at the end. I turn to see her cover her face.

I close the distance between us. It only takes three steps, but by the time my arms wrap around her, she's pushing me away. Her hands slam into my chest. She tries to knock me back, but only manages to throw herself off balance instead.

I grip her hip to steady her, but she slaps me. Hard across the face and the sting catches me by surprise.

I flex my jaw as she screams at me to get out. Her body's shaking. The sinful mix of hatred and betrayal ring in the air between us.

"Do you really want me out?" I ask her, genuinely not knowing anymore. I don't know at what point I lost her completely. There's only so many times I can ask her to give me everything while I hold back.

I guess I should be more surprised it hasn't happened sooner. I rub my jaw as I take a step back, only giving her the bit of space I'm willing to offer. "I know you still love me," I tell her and watch as she rips her eyes from me and takes a step back. Her face is blotchy and red and her breathing is frantic.

But she calms as she stands there not able to answer me. And that's all I needed. Just a little bit. Please, Kat. Just hold on a little while longer.

"Just tell me the truth," she begs me and I wish I could. I feel my throat tighten and my body tense. My hands clench as I swallow.

"I didn't sleep with her," I say and even I don't believe my words. But it's not what she thinks. I wish I could tell her, but the moment she finds out, everything will be at risk.

"Why don't I believe you?" she asks me and I don't have the decency to answer.

"I swear, Kat."

"So you've never slept with her?" she asks me and I know it's over. Her expression changes and her eyes darken when the silence stretches too long. So many secrets have built up. Too many to hide. She was never supposed to know. "Since we've been married," I start to say, knowing I'm toeing the line of truth. "I've never slept with anyone. Never kissed anyone but you." I look her in the eyes so she can see it's the truth. "The day I put that ring on your finger, it was only you."

"Then why put me through this?" she asks me with tears

in her eyes. "And what were you doing?" I struggle to keep my breathing calm as the questions start piling up.

I lick my dry lips and take a step forward. "Things got out of hand."

The words stop and I run my hands down my face.

"Why were you with her?" Kat asks me and I know she wants an answer right now.

"Because it's what I had to do," I tell her the truth with my eyes closed.

"What you had to do? You had to go to her hotel at three in the morning?" I can't look at her as I nod my head. "And you couldn't tell me this before?" I nod my head again.

"You tell me everything right now, or you leave."

"Another ultimatum?" The words drip with disdain.

"Don't talk to me like that," she says and I can hear her resolve harden.

"It's better if you didn't know everything," I say softly.

"Are you serious right now? You're throwing away our marriage over her? Over your job?"

"Kat, just-" I start to say, but she cuts me off.

“Fuck you,” she sneers and says, “I said get out.”

“I’m not leaving,” I tell her firmly, staring back at her, even as she turns her back to me.

“It doesn’t matter, the weekend’s coming,” she says beneath her breath as she leaves me.

I keep my feet planted as she stomps up the stairs and I wait for more. I wait for her to push me out, to yell at me, to demand more from me. I’m ready to fight, ready for war with her to keep her. But that’s not what I get.

She gives me back exactly what I gave her. *Nothing.*

CHAPTER 13

Kat

I hear your voice in my head,
It keeps me up at night.
It's rough and deep and sounds so sweet,
There's nothing left save that to fight.

The one that sounds like sorrow,
The one that sounds like pain.
Please just leave me behind,
I promise, there's nothing left to gain.

Four manuscripts to go through this weekend.

Four authors waiting to hear back from me.

I doubt I'll be able to focus enough to comprehend a full page. I've been reading this paragraph over and over and not a damn sentence is staying with me.

It doesn't matter though. None of this really does.

I'll stay in this room for as long as Evan's here. He's like a ghost in this house. A ghost of his former self.

So I'll do what I always do, I'll bury myself in work. That was the plan anyway, but I can't focus on anything but the sounds of him moving through the house.

He keeps walking by the door and I know he wants to open it, he wants me to talk to him, but all I can hear is him saying it'd be better if I didn't know. Fuck that and fuck him.

I'm not going to give him all of me when he can't be bothered to do the same.

So we're at a standstill, him refusing to leave and me refusing to forgive.

His voice plays in my head over and over again, telling me it's only ever been me. I want to believe it. It's everything I've been praying for him to say.

But then what is he hiding?

My eyes flicker to the screen as my nails tap on the

ceramic mug next to my laptop. Tick, tick, tick. I read the line over and over.

Love is a stubborn heart.

Magdalene, the editor, highlighted the line. She thinks it's beautiful and wants repetition of the analogy throughout the book.

Love is a stubborn heart.

Is it though? My forehead scrunches as I think back to the story in the manuscript. The tale about a modern-day Romeo and Juliet. Two families who hated each other and their children who wanted nothing more than to run away together. It's not a tragedy though, and it doesn't have a happily ever after either. It's too realistic.

If love really was that stubborn, wouldn't they have been together in the end?

Or maybe it wasn't really love. Or maybe love just wasn't enough.

I don't know that I agree that love is stubborn. I suppose it is, but more than that, it's stealthy and lethal. I nod my head at the thought.

Love is deadly.

I don't know the very moment I fell in love with Evan. It felt like I was counting the days until it would be over, and then one day, I simply decided on forever. Just like that. Slow, so slow and resistant, and then in an instant, I was his and he was mine. And that's how it was going to be forever.

I smile at the thought and try to focus on the lines on the computer. I try to read the words, but I keep glancing at the wall behind me. At a photo of the first night he took me to meet his parents.

I've never felt that kind of fear before. The fear of rejection. Not like that, because I'd never put my heart out there for anyone to take. And I was very much aware that Evan had every piece of me. Unless he didn't want me. In which case, I'd be broken and I didn't know how I'd recover.

The thought consumed me the night he brought me to his family home. I was sure his family wouldn't like me. It'd been so long since I'd been with a family for dinner. I used to go to my friend Marissa's when I was in high school. But it was just better not to.

When you lose your parents at fifteen, people tend to look at you as though they've never seen anything sadder. I'd rather be alone than deal with that.

And so I was, until Evan. And he didn't come on his own, he had a family that "had to meet me."

My back rests against the desk chair as I take in the photograph. I had it printed in black and white. It's the four of us on the sofa in his family home's living room. It's funny how I can see the colors of the sofa so clearly, the faded plaid, even though there isn't any color in the picture that hangs on my wall.

All four of us smiling. His mother insisted on taking the photo. Just as she'd insisted he bring me that night.

It's only now that I can remember how Evan's father looked at her. I didn't think anything of it at the time, but that's because they hadn't told us that she was sick.

I guess in some ways it was the last photograph. If that isn't accepting someone into your family, I don't know what is.

I have to sniffle as I think of her. I only met Marie twice. The first time was that night. The second was after she'd told Evan; she didn't have a choice, seeing as how she had to be hospitalized. The third time I saw her was at the funeral.

I may not know when I fell in love with him, but I think I know the moment he fell in love with me. The moment a part of his heart died and he needed something, or someone, to fill it. Maybe I got lucky that it was me. Or maybe it was a curse.

I roll my eyes as they water, hating that I'm stuck in the past because I can't move ahead with the future.

Maybe we weren't really meant to be. Maybe it was never the type of love that's meant to keep people together. Just the type of love when you feel compelled to give someone compassion.

Are there types of love? I find myself typing the question into the editor's suggestion box and then deleting it.

If there are, then maybe Evan's love is the stubborn kind. He's not so stubborn that he'll stay this weekend though. Come Friday he'll be gone again. Maybe it's a different love then …

It's only when I hear the bedroom door shut that I finally look back at the manuscript and email the editor back. I need more time before I can give feedback on any of these to the author and I'm ready to fall asleep in the corner chair, or anywhere I can where Evan will leave me alone.

I need more time for so much more. I need time and a clear head to move forward with my own life. I need someone to tell me I'm not walking away from the only man who will ever love me, but there's no email I can write for that unfortunate request.

CHAPTER 14

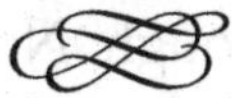

Evan

If I could focus on the hate and leave her all alone,
I'd be able to move forward, if only I had known.
I can't speak the truth, I don't want to make it real,
I can't stand what I've done or what it makes me feel.
Regret will settle in my chest and suffocate the day.
If only I could make it right, if only there was a way.

"It's good to see New York again," James says as I walk into his office on Greene Street in lower Manhattan.

He's staring out of the office window. It's a picture window, eight feet wide and eight feet in height, making the view seem like it's not quite real.

I don't return his sentiment. I'm fucking miserable. I want to drop to my knees and tell Kat everything. I think she'd forgive me. I can see it in her eyes that she wants to. I could tell her almost everything and I think she'd let me stay.

I'm too scared to do it though. Not until I end things here at least. It's step one to getting my Kat back.

"It's crazy how you miss it, isn't it?" he says as he turns to me. He's more relaxed than he was in London. I close the door as he takes a seat at the desk.

"Sorry you had to wait a minute, I was just getting this paperwork wrapped up." He sits back in his desk chair, loosening his tie and unfastening the top button of his crisp white dress shirt.

"Are we going to talk about it?" I ask him, needing to get this shit off my chest. I kept quiet in London, but I can't anymore. It's been weeks. That must be enough time.

Is that how long it takes to get away with murder?

"Talk about what?" he says and his voice is gravelly and low.

"Talk about the fact that the charges against Bruce are dropped?" I tell him and hold his cold gaze.

He may have been more relaxed before I sat down, but

now he's still. And silent. I let my eyes fall to the stack of papers on his desk, then to a small picture frame. It's a cube and matte black on all sides, and I have no idea who the woman in the picture is.

I absently pick it up, ignoring how his eyes bore into me, how his icy gaze heats as I let the question hang in the air, forcing him to answer.

The block is lighter than I thought it'd be and I don't recognize the woman. It's not his ex-wife, or his current girlfriend. Not that I thought Luna or whatever her name was, the fling of the month, would have a place in his office.

"My sister," James answers the unasked question. "A Christmas gift."

I nod my head once, putting the block back down and waiting for him to answer me.

"Bruce didn't do anything, so of course he got off," James says in an eerily calm voice. "We knew he was innocent." James pulls out a drawer and shuffles something inside of it, but I can't see what. He doesn't elaborate or give any room to further the conversation that we should have.

"What's done is done, and there's nothing more to say."

"That's not what Sam told me. She told me she's scared." It's the only reason I let her get so close. She's terrified that the truth is going to come out. And because she helped, she'd go down with me.

"Whose fault is that?" James sneers.

"She's your wife," I tell him, pushing the words out through my clenched teeth.

"I don't have a wife," he answers me with a sly smile, as if he's clean of this mess. As if it's all on me. And deep down in my gut, I know it is.

"Ex then," I tell him and add, "I didn't know the divorce had gone through yet." He picks up a pen and taps it against the desk but doesn't take his eyes off me. It hasn't gone through yet. All the money needs to be split one way or the other, and neither him nor Samantha, his ex-partner in this business and future ex-wife, wants to take less than the other.

"Either way, what's done is done and the two of you need to let it die."

"An innocent man-"

"Got off!" He looks me in the eyes as he leans forward and adds, "And a guilty man got away."

"We should have come forward."

"Should have, but you listened to a shady bitch. That's your problem, not mine."

My gaze falls to the desk as my fingers itch to form a fist. I called him. *His* office. But she's the one who answered.

"I panicked," I start to say, but he cuts me off.

"Because you fucked up. And now I have to clean up your mess and make sure you stay out of trouble."

"Is that what this is? You doing me a favor?" I ask sarcastically, letting the memory of that night fade and changing the conversation. I can't quit while there's still an investigation. I can't bring more attention to myself or to the company.

I wish I could tell Kat everything. But then she'd know she was married to a murderer. Even if it was just an accident. I'm a coward and I'll never be a man she deserves. But every day that goes by, I want to be more of the man I was the day before it all changed.

"I need time off," I tell him, fed up with the conversation. I imagine this isn't the first time something like this has happened and I sift through the memories of all the shit that's gone on behind the scenes for years. I never questioned anything, I never suspected a thing. Not until James brought me into the inner circle.

"Then I want to quit," I tell him as my fingers dig into the chair. The only thing I can think about is Kat. She'll get over that I kept this from her. I know she will. It's not the first time I've kept a secret from her. We'll be okay as long as I quit.

His thin lips twist into a half smile as he says, "Well that can't happen." He looks at me with a calculated glint in his eyes. Like he's been waiting for this and he's ready for my rebuttal, eager for it even.

"And why not?" I ask him as my muscles coil. "I don't want to work for this company anymore."

"That's not-"

"It's called quitting," I spit back at him. I don't need this job, since I've got plenty of money in the bank and Kat's career is finally stable. She bled money for years, but it's leveling out. We'll be alright financially and this is what she wants and what I need.

"You can't just quit; we have a contract."

"I can, and I am."

James' smile fades and he tilts his head to the side, an expression of the utmost sympathy on his wrinkled face. His brown eyes look darker as he picks up a folder on the left side of his desk. It wasn't hidden, but it's not labeled and it looks like all the rest.

My eyes follow his movement and my brow furrows until he opens it.

"The hotel had cameras. And of course they're gone now, but a few snapshots were taken. Some I think you'd find particularly interesting. Maybe enough so to stay."

I can imagine what they are before he flips the folder open. The eight-by-ten glossy photo paper shows the one thing that proves I lied. I'm walking into the hotel lobby I claimed I didn't enter. And I'm not alone. Standing right next to me is Tony. Only hours before he was found dead in the rec room of the hotel. The one reserved for our company and the division Bruce is the head of. Seeing Tony and his bloodshot eyes takes me back to that night. To the moment I found him dead on the floor.

My limbs freeze in waves. Like the betrayal that moves through me.

"It's just a security net on my end," James says and then closes the folder, pulling it off the desk and into his lap.

His prized possession. My heart thuds in my chest. The one out I thought I could take so I could hide from everything that's happened, slips away from me.

"So if I quit," I start to ask, but instead I just stop and stare ahead out of the window. I want to kill him. There's never been a time in my life when I've desired someone dead. But right now, it's all I want.

"Then I assume it's for less than moral reasons," James spells it out for me. "I need to protect myself."

"That's bullshit," I tell him and my words are hard. My hands turn to fists as they tremble with the need to get this anger out.

"I know, trust me I know," James says. "And I don't like this any more than you do."

A sarcastic huff of a laugh leaves me. "Fuck off," I sneer at him.

I stand up from the office chair so quickly it nearly falls over. I grip it so tight I think I'll break it. Fuck, I want to break it. I can picture beating the piss out of him with the broken wood.

My body is hot, my mind in a daze of regret and sickness.

"I'm leaving," I barely speak as I turn my back to him and start to walk off.

"The fuck you are," he seethes.

My body whips around, tense and ready to let it all out. Every day it's been building and building, the tension winding tighter and the need to destroy something climbing higher and higher. I only took a few steps away, and with his words I'm right back across the desk, ready to do something stupid.

My body heats as my fist moves from the chair to the desk and I lean closer. He may not want to show it, but I see the fear in his eyes.

He should be scared. He's fucking with me. Threatening me. No one is going to take my wife from me. I won't allow it.

"I need to get away from this. From you."

I never should have listened to him. He set me up. He used that night to his advantage and I played right into his hand.

It takes everything in me not to reach across the desk and haul him up by his collar. To fist the fine cloth in my grip and spit in his face.

Pure rage and adrenaline pump through my blood.

"Careful now," James smiles as he says it, but I notice how he leans back. Both of us know he's scared. If I throw this punch, if I push, he could bring it all to light.

And then I'll lose her forever.

"I'm going home, and I'll let you know when I'm available again." *Never.* The word is whispered in the back of my head. I'm never returning to this office. I'm never doing another thing for this fucker.

"You can't leave me. I'll ruin you," he practically whispers with nothing but hate. He says the words I already know.

"Ruin me then," I tell him, looking into his dark eyes as I turn the doorknob and leave him behind me. On the surface I'm calm, but brewing just beneath my skin is nothing but chaos. Everything I've feared has finally come.

Proof I was there.

Proof I lied.

I leave the office with the threat echoing in my head. I did this to myself, digging the hole deeper and deeper.

There's no way Kat will stay when it all goes down. I knew this day would come but I thought if I just didn't say it out loud, it would all go away.

Wishful thinking.

The day of reckoning is coming.

CHAPTER 15

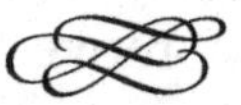

Kat

Never trapped, never alone,
This city never sleeps.
Even in the daylight,
The sins are left to creep.
They tempt me and pull me,
And make me feel alive.
My mouth is dry, my body hot.
In temptation regrets will thrive.

My iPhone lights up as I push the top button and check the time again, and then the date. I'm anxious for this meeting and I'm not usually like this. But then again, I'm anxious all the time now.

Evan hasn't come home; he isn't talking to me. It's been four days and each day I feel like I need to cave more and more. I just need him back.

A huff leaves me and I shake my head at the thought. Breakups are always hard, but that's what this is and there's only one way to move on and that's to get it over with.

I don't want to be in our townhouse, but I have nowhere else to go and I can't sleep. I didn't know how much I wanted him there until he was gone. Maybe it's because it was his own decision. Maybe that's why it hurts so much.

An easy breath leaves me as I stand behind the only woman in line at Brew Madison and tilt my head to read the sign on the back wall. All they have to offer is written in chalk, although the large, glass-covered shelves house all the treats they have available. From small pastries to toasted breakfast sandwiches, there's something for everyone.

I haven't had much of an appetite either, but every sip of my coffee this morning made me nauseated, so a blueberry muffin top it is.

The brunette curls of the woman in front of me swing from side to side as she talks. I can't see her face, but I know she's young. From her bright red high heels and black leather jacket paired with white shorts a bit too short for fall, she's definitely a downtown girl.

I smile at the thought as she waits for her coffee, pumpkin spice.

I used to be like her. Stylish and in charge of my destiny. New to the city and ready to tame it.

And my God, I thought I had.

A career and reputation in this publishing industry that I reached within only a few years. I'm an agent worth my weight in gold and everyone knows it. A man who still drips of sex appeal and has an edge to him that is irresistible. A townhouse near Madison Square Garden. Even if it is small, it's the closest we could get. And it's New York, so location is *everything*.

And my closet … the girl in front of me would kill for my closet. Not that she would know it based on how I'm dressed now.

My name had a purpose and strength to it that made me proud. Evan and I were a powerhouse in the social scene. The couple everyone wanted to be. But envy comes with threats and in its nature, ruins.

In the last few years, the highs of this world have crashed.

And I let it. I spent my life not living it, wanting more

and more from my work. Running as fast as I could, just to stay still while I ignored every other change in the world around me. How could I not have seen it deteriorating?

As the woman turns and I get a look at her cateye makeup that's subtle enough to still be businesslike and red lips that match her heels, I remember that feeling that used to flow through me. The one that said I could conquer anything.

Yeah, I used to be like her. I still have the heels and even the stylish clothes, although I lean toward professional and those shorts sure as shit don't say that.

"What can I get you?" the young man asks me from behind the counter. He's got to be in his early twenties at most. I catch a glimpse of his sleeve tattoo and it reminds me of Evan's for only a moment.

"A chai and a blueberry muffin," I answer him and reach for my card in my wallet. It's a Kate Spade and the soft pink and white match the purse, but I'm only just now realizing that it looks a bit dingy. Not so much so that it's noticeably dirty. But enough where it doesn't look so new anymore.

As I wait for my chai, I look at my reflection in the glass. I guess the same can be said about me. My fingers tease my hair at the roots, putting a little more volume there and I apply a coat of stain on my lips.

I wrap the belt around my shirt a little tighter, showing off my waist and lean to my right in the reflection.

I'm not done yet. There's still life in me. There's still that girl who wanted more buried deep down inside. But what exactly she wants more of remains a question.

Evan, the silent answer, is obvious.

But instead the voice in my head whispers love.

Even if he can't give it to me. It's what I'm desperate for. To love and be loved.

The bells to the door chime as I accept my chai and muffin top. I silently pray that it's not Jacob so I can have a moment to try to shove this down.

No such luck.

I smile broadly when I see him, hiding everything I was just thinking and focusing on him and his career. And how much work we both need to do to get his branding both going in the right direction and noticed by the right market.

"Jacob," I greet him and his green eyes focus on me.

"Katherine, it's wonderful to finally have a one-on-one,"

he says as he steps over the welcome mat and slips off his thin, black wool jacket. He has a downtown style that would pair well with the woman who was just here. From his gray shirt that hangs low but is fitted tight across his chest, to the boyish grin and messy dark hair.

"It is, thank you so much for meeting me here," I talk awkwardly as I make my way to the front of the shop, making sure not to spill the hot drink in my hand.

"Finally meeting my new agent," he says with a hint of something I can't place.

"I hope so," I answer sweetly.

"The rain this fall is ridiculous," Jacob says as he runs his hand over his hair and then wipes it off on his worn jeans.

His white Chuck Taylor sneakers squeak on the floor as he takes a step closer to me. His expression is comical. With both hands full, one of chai and the other with the muffin top, I gesture to the table where I already have my laptop set up. "Right over here," I tell him and put both the chai and the muffin to the left side of my computer before turning around to face him.

I have to crane my neck. "You're so much taller in person," I tell him and hold out a hand for a handshake. His right hand engulfs mine and his shake is firm.

The grin on his face grows to a wide smile and his perfect teeth flash back at me.

He's damn good looking and the fact that his face isn't anywhere on his profiles or brand is a mistake.

"You are too good looking for every one of your readers not to see your face," I tell him as we both take a seat. "I know this is a meeting to see if you're interested in coming on board and if our goals align, but the way I like to approach things is to treat you like a client from the start so you know what you're getting."

"I like to know what I'm getting, so let's dive in. What do you want from me, Katherine?" Jacob asks me and for a split second, a thought enters my mind.

It's only a fraction of a second. A glimpse of his mouth on mine, his hands on my body. Pushing me against the wall like Evan did only a few nights ago.

Thankfully, it vanishes before I can show any admission of what I was thinking.

I focus on the plan I have laid out for him and turn the computer around on the table.

"We're going to start with your strong points, which obviously is your writing, and then work our way into other aspects of marketing and social media that I think you're ignoring so we can come up with a plan that you're comfortable with, but also one that will work."

The words come out of my mouth smoothly even though my mind's racing.

It's been a while since I've looked at a man and thought the things running through my head. I tell myself it's because I'm looking for comfort. Looking for someone to desire me like Evan does.

So I don't feel trapped and alone.

"Lead the way, Miss Thompson."

I shake my head, ready to correct him, ready to tell him it's *Mrs.* Thompson. But I don't. In fact, I find myself hiding my left hand behind the computer.

It's only because the attention is nice.

A distraction, a sweet voice whispers in the back of my head as I smile at Jacob and hit the right arrow on the keyboard to move to the first point I want to make.

I could never do that, I tell myself. But I leave my hand where it is and when he tells me goodbye, again calling me miss, I still don't correct him.

CHAPTER 16

Evan

She makes my blood heat,
My breathing tense and ragged.
Love's not a straight line,
It's reckless and it's jagged.
Beyond the lust, beyond desire,
There's something in its wake.
It's jealousy that makes me weak,
It's hate that makes me break.

Brew Madison is my wife's favorite place in this whole damn city. My shoes smack on the wet pavement and rain spits from the sky as I close the door a block down and make my way toward the coffee shop.

For years she's come here. She and Jules used to write together in the corner. Jules was her first client here in New York. It's how she met her now close friend. I huff and the breath turns to steam as I stride toward the entrance and peek in through the glass window.

It used to be a habit of mine to stop here before going home when I landed. Nine times out of ten, she'd be in the back corner, immersed in a book.

But then things changed. She stopped going out and I stopped searching for her. I knew she'd be home, stuck in her office and working no matter what time of day it was.

I had to make sure nothing was going to happen when I left James' office. I couldn't go home and have the cops come for me there. I wouldn't put her through that.

But days have passed, and I miss her. I'm dying without her.

Just before I get to the glass door, I spot my wife. But more importantly, I see who she's with.

Some asshole is with her. I'm sure he's just a client, but as they walk toward the exit, Kat's eyes on her purse as she rummages through it, looking for her keys I'd think, his eyes are all over her body.

The bastard licks his lower lip, and his gaze flickers to Kat's breasts and then to her eyes as she peeks up at him.

She smiles so naively and tucks her hair behind her ear, but what stops the anger and the possessiveness running through me, is the blush that rises to her cheeks. My body goes cold and my feet turn to cement standing outside of the shop, watching the two of them unknowingly walk toward me.

She knows he's looking. She knows he likes what he sees. And she's letting him.

The chill that runs through my body fuels something deep inside of me. Something primal and raw. The rain that crashes down on me as the clouds roll in and the sky turns darker by the second does nothing to calm the rage growing inside of me.

I open the door just as the two of them are leaving. My grip on the handle is tight and unforgiving as I wait for them to look up at me.

Kat doesn't stop talking, her sweet voice rattling off something about a signing and what needs to be purchased.

He sees me first, his eyes widening slightly as he takes in my expression. His first instinct is to angle his body, putting himself between me and my wife. It pisses me off and I force my body to stay still, keeping myself from shoving him away from her.

My teeth grind against one another as I stare at his hand, still on her lower back as if he has any right to touch her.

“Evan,” Kat looks up at me surprised at first, without a hint of anything other than shock, but instantly her expression changes. “What are you doing? You’re getting soaked!” she admonishes me in front of the fucker still standing too close.

Pride flows through me as she pulls me into the coffee shop, even if she’s doing it out of frustration.

She looks from my wet shoulders and the rain dripping down my hair to my forehead and back and then glances outside the shop. She hasn’t even acknowledged the man she’s with. Her small hands focus on wiping off as much water as she can as she positions me over the large welcome mat at the front of the store.

“Nice to meet you,” I say to the man eyeing the two of us. “I’m Kat’s husband.”

Kat looks up at me and bites her tongue.

“Didn’t know she was married,” the fucker says and I read him loud and clear. I knew there was a crack in my marriage. But this shit isn’t something I’m going to take easily. It takes everything in me not to be aggressive toward this shithead.

She turns a bright shade of red, but instead of defending us and our relationship, instead of taking my side, she says the worst thing she could to me right now.

"I don't know what we are right now," she says more to me than to him as she looks me in the eyes, daring me to say another word. When I'm quiet, she turns to him.

"I'm sorry for the interruption, Jacob."

"Jake, you can call me Jake," he says to her and doesn't even bother to look at me. The awkward tension heats.

"I'll touch base with you after I get the schedule drawn up, and make sure you get me those summaries as soon as you're able to."

Jake nods his head at Kat and then looks at me to say, "Nice to meet you." He doesn't take his time leaving, not with the rain now coming down in sheets.

"You don't know what we are?" I ask her, feeling the rage wane as the sound of the door closing and the battering of the rain quiets again.

"When you make an ass out of yourself in front of a client, what do you expect me to do?" she hisses.

The rain gets harder and louder as we stand off to the

side of the entrance. I take a look around and there are only two other people in the entire place. Both of them women who look like they're on a lunch break, dressed for office jobs. One on each side of the room, both of them on their phones and one with headphones in her ears.

"We can wait it out. Get a cup of coffee?" I ask her.

At first Kat looks up at me like I'm crazy. Maybe I am.

"And do what?" she asks. "Play let's-keep-a-secret and hide-away-for-days?"

I ignore her brutal tone and take a chance, wrapping my arm around her waist.

She jumps back for a second, but only because I'm soaking wet.

I chuckle at her response, deep and rough and it makes her smile. She's quick to hide it, but it's there.

"I know you're mad at me," I tell her softly. "I don't want to make you angry, Kat. I love you, and I'm trying."

The trace of all humor fades and she peeks up at me and whispers, "I wish you wouldn't."

I brush the hair from her face and smile down at her as I tell her, "I'll never stop fighting for you."

At my words, she pushes away from me and says, "Then let's talk until the rain lets up." She looks over her shoulder and out of the window, as if checking to see if our time is already up.

We head to the back corner of the shop. The rest of the seating in the place is all high-top tables and bar-height seats, but in the corner is an L-shaped booth. The same shiny white tabletop, but the seating is for customers who want to spend a while in here and that's what I need with her right now, more time.

She doesn't look at me as she tosses her purse into the booth and then fishes out her wallet.

"You like him?" I ask her, feeling small pieces of my heart crumble off. Kat's eyes narrow as she huffs out a breath of frustration.

"Knock it off," she tells me and I feel torn. I saw the look in her eyes. She's a natural flirt and so am I, but I know she liked the attention more than she should. She felt comfortable with it.

"I don't like him."

"Good to know," she answers me immediately, crossing her arms as she walks toward the counter to order something.

I follow her, like a lost fucking puppy. "I mean it, he

wants you, Kat," I tell her and then nearly flinch from the look in her eyes. "I don't want anyone else's hands on you."

"It was innocent."

"The fuck it was," I bite back instantly. I don't give her a chance to speak.

"You can't look me in the eyes and tell me you didn't like it." The air between us turns hot instantly.

"He's a client," she says beneath her breath. My eyes dart from her to the man behind the counter. As soon as I look at him, he averts his eyes, pretending like he didn't just hear the venom in Kat's voice.

"Client or not," I say, standing my ground but all it does is wind Kat up more.

"I'm not the one keeping secrets and lying, I'm not the one who's breaking up this marriage," she says much lower, so much so that it sounds like it was hard for her to even get the words out.

"Stop it," I tell her and grip her hip as she tries to walk past me, back to the booth and undoubtedly to get her stuff and leave.

"I'm sorry," I whisper in her ear and hold her closer to me. I splay my hand on her lower back, feeling the tension in her body slowly leave her.

I could fight this, but it's not worth it to upset her. I wait, giving her a moment to calm down and forget about that asshole. For now.

I say a silent prayer when she walks back to the table.

I sit back in the seat, watching the steam rise from her cup as she slips the lid off and grabs a packet of sugar from the center of the table.

The packet makes a flapping sound as she shakes it back and forth between her forefinger and thumb to get the sugar down. The motion is forceful and she stares at it as she does it, before finally ripping it open and dumping the sugar into the cup.

"I don't tell you everything." The words slip out as the need to win her back takes over everything else.

She's still for a moment, waiting for more.

"It's not like I do anything that's … that I want to hide from you. You know what it's like when I go to work."

"I know," Kat says with zero trace of a fight in her voice. "I remember."

"I loved it when you came out with me. You know that, right?"

She finally looks up at me, but only for a moment before she nods her head then slips on the cap to her coffee cup.

"I don't have time for that kind of … stuff anymore."

I love that her mind immediately went to the thought of me asking her to come with me. At the beginning of this year, that's all I wanted from her. So we could spend more time together and I could show her off. But the answer was always no, so I just stopped asking. My heart thumps hard in my chest, remembering how we got into a fight over it a few months back.

"I gave my notice," I tell her and her eyes fly to mine, looking accusing more than anything. "Because you wanted me to," I say the words as if they're the truth and for a moment it feels like they are. But then I remember that's not the reason. I remember what happened. I remember everything in a flood and I have to turn away to breathe in deep and focus on keeping Kat. That's the only thing I care about while everything else collapses around me.

"I just regret a lot of the things I've done this year and maybe for a while now-"

"For a while?" Kat repeats and her eyes reflect the pain that's in her voice.

"I didn't cheat on you, Kat," I say immediately. "It's not

what you think," I tell her and feel like a liar. Because I am one. "I told you, you're the only one for me."

Before I can say anything else, she shakes her head and that false smile mars her face. "I don't know what you did. But I don't want to know anymore," she says quietly, staring at the cup in her hands before looking back up at me. "We're different people and I think it was only a matter of time before something like this ..." her voice cracks, but she doesn't cry. She simply looks away.

My heartbeat slows. So slow that it's painful.

"Where are you sleeping tonight?" Kat asks me and I have to swallow the spiked lump deep down in my throat before I can answer.

"You don't want me to come home?"

"It would be easier if you didn't."

"Easier for what?" I ask her.

"Easier for the breakup, Evan." Her lips part and then she wavers to add, "It's not about love anymore or about what we had. It's about trust and what we've become. I need a fresh start and a life I'm proud of. And I don't think it includes you in it."

"It does," I answer her instantly. "And I want the same."

She stares back at me with an expression that shows how

vulnerable she is. How much she wants to believe what I'm telling her.

I take her hand in mine and tell her, "I'll do whatever you want, so long as when it's all said and done I get to keep you."

I stare in her eyes knowing I've never said anything more truthful, but also knowing that's not how this story will end.

CHAPTER 17

Kat

Makeup kisses taste so sweet,
Lost in lust and succumbed to the heat.
Your soft moan makes me forget,
I ignore the anger, the sadness, the threat.

The bed groans and dips as I turn back onto my right shoulder, pushing the pillow between my knees and trying to sleep.

I've been alone all my life. Until Evan, anyway. When he first started sleeping over, it was hard to fall asleep. Unless he fucked me to the point of exhaustion, which was often.

You'd think it'd be easy going back to being alone. I was a

pro at it for years and worse yet, I was proud of it. The train goes by and the sound cuts through the white noise of the city. The windows are closed, but I still hear it. I can even feel the rumble and vibrations as I try to lie still on the bed. And that's when I get a whiff of Evan's scent. When I'm alone, missing him, I sleep on his side of the bed. It's easiest the first night he's gone. It smells just like him. Each day it gets a little harder and working late nights gets more appealing. But even the masculine scent that drifts toward me as I inch my head closer to his pillow isn't enough to comfort me. And why would it? I'm losing him and everything we had.

I toss the heavy comforter off my body and sit up, wiping the sleep from my eyes and dangling my feet over the side of the bed. It's nearly 1 a.m. and pitch black in the room. I should be sleeping, considering the fatigue plaguing my body and conscious it should come easy.

My fingers run through my long hair, separating it and braiding it loosely before I take a sip of water from the glass on the nightstand. If I get up and start working, I know I won't sleep at all tonight. The very thought makes my heart thump harder. Work is killing me, lack of sleep is destroying me. But both are because I'm completely and utterly alone.

Just breathe. I let my head fall back and slowly creep back under the covers. All I need to do is breathe.

But that hope is short-lived as I hear Evan climb the stairs. I had one condition to him coming home, and that was leaving me the bedroom. Which he said he wasn't going to do, and that offer went off the table.

Even if it hurts me, I'd rather feel pain in his absence than a fraction of that pain in his presence.

I close my eyes as I hear the door open. For a moment I think I should pretend to be asleep. But I don't want any more lies in our relationship. Whatever our relationship even is now.

"I thought you were going to your dad's? Or a hotel?" I ask him and then hold my breath. I should want him to leave. That's what a sane woman who's getting a divorce should want. But there isn't an ounce of me that wants to see him walk out that door.

"I was going to," Evan says and then slips his shirt off over his head. He keeps his eyes on me, daring me to say something, but my eyes focus on his broad chest.

In five years his body has changed, as has mine. But he's still lean and muscular. My body heats and my thighs scissor slightly, but I play it off, turning my back to him to lie on my left shoulder.

"Is that alright?" he asks me, his voice carrying through the dark night and cutting me down to my deepest insecurity. It's not alright and nothing about this situation is. But those aren't the words that come out of my mouth.

My eyes squeeze shut tight and I give in to what I want. Wouldn't it be a lie to deny it?

"I'm afraid I'll like it too much if you stay," I tell him with my eyes closed as the bed dips. I don't watch him as I lay out all the bare truth. "I'm afraid I'll forgive you and I'll forget why we shouldn't be married." My breath comes in staggered hiccups. All the words pouring out from deep down in my soul and leaving my lips in a rush.

A rough sound comes from deep in his throat as the bed dips. "You don't know what you want, Kat," Evan tells me although the confidence is missing. "You want me to leave because you're afraid. You won't fight for me to stay because you know I will regardless of what you say, isn't that right?"

My brow furrows as I take in his words. I can see his eyes in the dark room, staring deep into mine as he climbs closer to me, making the bed shift beneath my still body. He stares at me as if I'm his prey and that's just how I feel. "No. I want you to leave because we're leading different lives." I have to second-guess my words.

"Then let's get back on track. Let's start over," he whispers and then leans closer to me. As if checking his boundaries as he rests his hand on the pillow above my head. I don't push him away, but I don't move toward him either.

I'm fucked no matter what I do.

I feel empty and hollow. All the sadness and regret has been shed from me, leaving nothing behind but faint memories of what we had and the hint of all the hopes and dreams I had so long ago to make my heart flutter. As I close my eyes and swallow the lump in my throat, Evan lies next to me, gently resting his hand on my hip. He's silent but I can hear his steady breath and that smell. I inhale deeper. God, what that smell does to me. My head dips further into the pillow as I readjust under the covers and when I do, Evan lifts his hand slightly. Waiting to see which way I'll turn.

And I turn toward him.

"You make me a stupid woman," I tell him as my eyes slowly open. His hazel eyes are so clear at this angle. Maybe it's the moon creeping in from the slit between the curtains. Or maybe something else.

He smirks at me, although there's a sadness in his smile as he brushes my hair from my face.

"Tell me you'll stay with me."

"Tell me why I shouldn't," I say back instantly and the soft look of longing in his eyes fades away and the soothing motion of his thumb rubbing along my temple falters. My eyes drop to his chest and my heart drops to the pit of my stomach. "You said you didn't cheat," I tell him, but mostly I make a promise to myself. "So I believe you."

"Thank you," he says so softly beneath his breath I hardly hear him. His shoulders sag slightly and it makes the bed creak with relief.

I want to say more. I want to make some sort of demand or ultimatum ... or ask why he was there. Why he lied to the world. But instead I curl into him.

"Don't leave me," he gives me the request and wraps his arms around me, pulling me closer to him, closer to his scent, his warmth, to the man I've been desperate to be with for so damn long.

"I won't promise you that," I tell him with my eyes open, staring at a small scar on his left shoulder. I lift my hand up and let my fingers play along it. "You're right that I don't know what I want. So we'll just have to find out."

He's quiet for a long time. And part of my heart, a very large part of it aches. It's a horrible feeling and it makes my eyes sting. But I won't mourn what I'm not even sure I've lost yet. It's just the threat of ending something I've valued so dearly and for so long that hurts.

My shoulders shake slightly as I take in a shuddering

breath, and that's when he cups my chin and forces me to look at him.

"You know I love you," he says with a ragged breath. "More than anything, anything in the world," he says as he shakes his head.

I sniffle and try to ignore how the pain grows. "I do," I tell him and then try to hide my face, but his grip on my chin is too strong and I can only close my eyes, feeling the smallest bit of tears that threaten to spill over soak into my lashes.

"Don't cry, Kat," Evan whispers as he rests his forehead against mine. "I love you, and that's all that matters." For some reason it seems so obvious to me in this moment that those words were more for him than they were for me. My eyes open to see his closed. To see the pain there. To see how desperate he is.

And that's what I can blame it on. It's my undoing.

It always has been. He needs me, and I crave it.

"Kiss me-" Before I can get the command off my lips, his are on mine. Devouring me and taking every little piece I'm willing to give. And I crumble underneath him. My hands fly to his hair as he deepens the kiss. The air turns hotter as my skin heats and our breathing quickens.

"Kat," he barely breaks away from me to whisper my

name and then presses his lips harder against mine as he grabs my hips and pulls me toward him.

My gasp is muted as his tongue dives into my mouth. My back arches and my breasts push against his hard chest as he climbs on top of me.

Every second I'm acutely aware that I'm falling backward. It pains my heart as I pull away from him, digging my head into the pillow to feel the cool air. But I can't stop this. I never could. He nips along my neck and my pussy clenches with need as my legs wrap around his waist.

My heels dig into his ass while I close my eyes tight and let my body do what it wants. It's only ever wanted him. And I won't deny my needs.

Not when he worships my body like this, kissing his way down my body as he strips the clothes from me. The only sound is our breathing as I cautiously open my eyes to watch.

His fingertips brush against my skin as he takes off the last piece and stares at my glistening sex.

"So fucking wet for me." He says the words out loud, although I don't think they were for me. Another time, I'd blush. But there's no shame or embarrassment right now. It's desperation.

He parts from his clothes faster than I can steady my breath. The moonlight casts shadows on his chiseled chest and makes my clit throb with need. My eyes are drawn to his hands as he strokes his length. And then he does it again and I can't help how my lips part with desire and my legs spread wider. My body's ready, willing and aching for him to take me.

"I'm the only one who can satisfy you like this, Kat." My gaze shifts to Evan as he looks me in the eyes. Holding my gaze as he adds, "Don't ever forget that."

I can't respond, I don't have time. In one swift motion he's buried to the hilt inside of me. Stretching my walls and sending a spike of heat, desire and bit of pain through me. My skin lights on fire as a strangled scream tears through me.

It's nothing but pleasure as he stills deep inside of me. Waiting for me to adjust to his girth as he kisses his way back up my waist to my collarbone and then my lips.

The kisses are softer now. Small pecks and nips until I open my eyes and he brings them to a halt.

"I love you," he whispers and then moves slowly. My legs wrap around his waist and my fingers move to his shoulders as he moves slowly at first. Burying his head into my neck before I can tell him the same.

He rocks his hips, his rough pubic hair rubbing against my clit with each small movement and bringing me higher and higher. The climax feeling so close but so far away just the same.

I can only make small whimpers as he speeds up, knowing he's going to send me crashing to my release. All the while he rides through my orgasm, fueled by my cries of pleasure. I cling to him for dear life as my body seems paralyzed and he continues to take from me. Pounding into me, harder and harder. Pistoning his hips until the headboard smacks against the wall in rhythm with his relentless thrusts.

CHAPTER 18

Evan

The regrets, the guilt, the shame,
So many sins to try and tame.
Each one darker, each one worse,
Living life as if it's cursed.
Until the day fate gave me her,
That was the day my past did blur.
And with her, I'd leave it all,
Just for her, my world will fall.

It's been a long damn time since I've made breakfast for Kat. It's probably been a year or more since we've even woken up together, that's how fucked our schedules have been.

I can hear her bare feet pad down the stairs as I set the

last plate on the table. It's fresh pineapple and strawberries I cut up. Bacon's still the prominent scent though. Bacon and eggs for breakfast. A plate of hotcakes and fruit in the center and of course, her coffee.

I grab her mug from her spot on the table. It's still burning hot but I make sure to put it handle out as I turn around to face her. Maybe I'm pussy whipped. Maybe I'm sucking up. Either way, I don't give a fuck.

The sight of her messy halo of hair and wide eyes with a bit of mascara still left over from yesterday makes my heart pump hard in my chest. She's got on nothing but a baggy Henley of mine and it makes her seem even more petite than she already is. My Kat's never been an early riser. Only when she has to, or apparently when the smell of breakfast is in the air.

She's gorgeous even when she's a mess.

"You have good timing," I tell her as she hesitantly grabs the coffee. I can see her shoulders sag just a bit and her eyes close as she takes in the smell though. And it gives me a sense of pride. Even if it's just for the moment.

"Good morning," she says with a soft smile, but it's barely hiding her true feelings. I force a smile back and pull out her chair.

"I don't know the last time I had an actual breakfast," she

says as she takes the seat and then looks up at me. "Thank you," she says. It's genuine, but with her shoulders hunched and that sad look in her eyes, I can't even give her a response.

I wish I could hold on to last night forever. But the sun had to rise, and I need to come clean to her. She deserves that much.

The chair legs scratch on the wooden floor as I pull out my seat. I grimace slightly and then clear my throat as I sit down, noticing how Kat doesn't seem to care. She's too tired, or maybe it's something else.

With both hands on her mug, she leans back in her seat and gives me a small smile but doesn't reach for any food. She doesn't say anything either. She's just waiting. And I wish I had something better to offer her than what's going to come out of my mouth.

"I want a fresh start … and the marriage we were supposed to have," I say out loud as I push the fork through the pancake on my plate, but I don't eat it. I feel sick to my stomach.

A heavy breath leaves me and I rub my forehead to get out some of the tension. I can't tell her everything, but I can give her something that has killed me for years; a truth I wish didn't exist.

My skin's hot and my throat's dry. It's been years, and I never intended on telling Kat. I didn't want her to know and it was before things changed for me. Before my mother told me she was dying. Before Kat came to me and showed me she was the person I needed in my life forever. It happened before I realized she was mine and I was never going to let her go.

"You okay?" Kat asks and there's genuine pain in her voice. Sadness and concern I wish weren't there. She's too good for me. I've made so many mistakes and this is going to crush her and hurt her more than it should. It meant nothing to me back then, but it'll mean everything to her right now. And I hate it.

"There's something I've got to tell you." As I say the words I look Kat in the eyes, and her face changes. She has this way of hiding her emotions, but it doesn't last long. She's looking at me with a hard stare and her lips pressed into a thin line. She gives it to me all the time, but I know the second I give her silence, that mouth will open and every emotion she's feeling will show. She can't hide it from me.

"When you asked me about Samantha, if I'd slept with her," I have to break off from my thought and take in another breath.

The clink of Kat's fork hitting the ceramic plate makes

my chest feel tight. She lets out a small sound, almost a sigh but weighted down with a bitter hopelessness.

"I told you the truth, that I haven't been with anyone since we got married," I say and watch her eyes, her expression, everything about her, but she doesn't look back at me. Her shoulders rise, like she's holding her breath and waiting for a bomb to go off.

"It was years ago, Kat. Before I knew how much you meant to me." The words come up my throat as if they're scratching and digging to stay buried down deep inside of me.

Her expression crumples the second I hint at the affair. If you can even call it that. "I felt like I was lying to you. Every. Single. Time." I bang my fist on the table and the plates rattle with each word and make Kat jump, but I can't help it. "I felt like a bastard when I looked you in the eyes and said nothing happened, because you should have already known."

"When?" Kat asks me.

"I swear that night in the papers was about something else. Something that has nothing to do with that woman or sleeping with her. It was-"

"When!" she screams out the question as her eyes gloss over. She doesn't stop staring at me, but the emotion I expect to see isn't there. It's only anger, a furious rage that stares back at me. "When did you sleep with her?"

"The night I got the call from my mother," I swallow thickly and add, "I was with her."

"The night she told you?" she asks me with a morbid tone and I nod, feeling that acid churn in my stomach as my clammy hands clench. "You were at the company party?" she asks instantly, although it's more of her recollecting than an actual question. She didn't even have to take a second to think about it. But I guess that night is something that will forever stay with both of us.

"You were supposed to take me out that night," Kat says and each word sounds sadder and sadder as she looks away from me. "You were fucking her while at work."

"It was a one-time thing. A mistake. I didn't know who she was and things were getting serious with us, Kat. You don't understand. It wasn't how it seems." I stumble over my words. Leaning closer to her and reaching for her, but she pushes away from the table, slamming her palms against it and scooting the chair back.

My hands fly into the air, keeping them up. As if I'm not a threat. Trying to keep her here with me to give me a chance to explain.

"Look, we were getting serious and I needed … I don't know how to explain it."

"You didn't want to be with me anymore so you went and slept with the first girl to bat her eyes at you?" she asks although it's an accusation and a bitter one at that.

I can't explain how pathetic I feel as she looks at me like I'm the devil. It was just a game back then. I wish I could change it. If I'd known what Kat would mean to me, I'd have put a ring on her finger the moment I laid eyes on her. I never would have done anything to risk what we had. *Lies. So many lies,* a voice whispers. If that was the truth, I wouldn't have needed to call Samantha with my eyes on a lifeless body in the corporate hotel room. If she knew everything, she'd hate me.

"I messed up and I made so many mistakes," I say and start to lean toward her and beg for mercy, but she's not having it.

"How many women have you fucked since I've been with you?" Her voice is hard and full of nothing but bitterness.

"Just her, just Samantha and just that once." I stare into her eyes, but she refuses to look at me. "Please, Kat," my voice begs her as I lean forward but she's quick to stand up, nearly toppling the chair over just so she can get away from me.

I deserve this. I deserve worse.

Regret consumes me. I wish I hadn't told her. Fuck. I don't know what to wish for anymore. I wasn't going to tell her about the coke and everything else. I thought that would be her breaking point. Not this.

I swallow thickly and try to remember everything else I was going to say. "It's why I feel so guilty about these allegations and why I didn't say anything to the press. I needed them to think it'd happened and it kind of did, just years ago."

"Why were you in the hotel lobby with her at three in the morning?" she asks me as she crosses her arms over her chest, bunching the shirt and finally letting her eyes fall on me.

I have to swallow the hard lump in my dry throat before I can answer her. "I needed an alibi," I tell her and feel like that much more of a lesser man.

"Are you fucking serious, Evan?" she spits out her words, looking at me with more disgust than I've ever seen on her face.

"I'm sorry. It was an accident."

"It's always an accident. Always a mistake. Why do you do this! Why do you put yourself in these situations!" She screams at me with a rage I know she's had pent up inside of her. I'm too old to be this stupid. I never should have continued working for James. But the money and the lifestyle were so addicting. And it was a high I couldn't refuse.

"I told you, I quit. I'm not going to put myself in-" As I shake my head, trying to get the words out, I can't remember a damn thing I'd planned on saying.

"It's too little, too late, Evan," Kat says and cuts me off.

She sneers at me before leaving me alone in the room, whipping around and not bothering to say another word. I watch her back as she storms up the stairs.

I've never felt this way before in my life. Like I've hurt the one person in the world who would never hurt me. Like I betrayed her. Like I'm not worth a damn thing.

And there's no way to make that right.

I don't know how to make any of this right.

CHAPTER 19

Kat

I knew the truth,
I didn't want to believe.
But deep in my gut,
The agony did seethe.
Call me a fool,
Say what you will.
But I can't help it,
I love him still.
That's why it hurts,
To say goodbye.
To make him leave,
I want to die.

I can't stop thinking about it. How Evan fucked her.

I should be focused on the fact that he needed an alibi. The fact that only weeks ago he was doing shit he knows is wrong and could send him to jail. But that's the man he's always been. I knew better than to turn a blind eye, but that's really what I've been doing, isn't it?

It's an odd feeling, like waking up from a long and deep sleep or having a blindfold taken off after wearing it for days. Has it always been this way?

I knew what kind of life he was leading and the risks that came with it. And I didn't do a damn thing about it. I should be ashamed, mortified.

And yet all I can think about is him fucking her.

And how many times I've seen her at events. Not once did she make it seem like anything had happened. She comes off sweet and innocent. She's petite like me but wears soft colors and always has perfectly manicured, pale pink nails. She looks like a little doll, prim and proper. I never would have expected it. I remember how genuinely happy she seemed when she gushed over my engagement ring.

That fucking bitch.

The door to my office opens behind me, the telltale creak making my eyes open and then narrow as I see his reflection on the black computer screen. I don't even know if the damn thing is on anymore. Or how long I've been sitting here. Staring at a worn spot on my desk and thinking about how he fucked her, knowing he was going to see me only hours later.

What would have happened if his mother hadn't chosen that moment to tell him to come home and that she wasn't well? Maybe that would have been the night he chose to break it off with me. After all, every day with him was like ticking off a check box. I knew it wasn't going to last. I was waiting for it to end.

Marie fucked me over.

"Kat," Evan says from behind me. Hearing him say my name makes a shudder run down my spine. It's a slow one that sends a chill over my body.

"I'm going to do everything I can to prove to you how much I love you."

"Do I even know you?" Even as I whip around and sneer at him a sick voice in the back of my head answers me. *Yes. Yes, you knew what you were doing. You knew the man you married.*

"You're the only one who does," he says, looking me in

the eyes as his broad shoulders fill the doorframe to my office. "You know I love you too."

I scoff at him, choosing to ignore the truth and how much I blame myself.

Right now, it's all on him. I didn't cheat on him. I didn't continue to live a lifestyle that was obviously going to tear us apart.

He did. And fuck him for that.

"I hate you right now." The words slip out in a breath and he visibly flinches.

"You're angry, and you have every right to be."

"Angry doesn't cut it!" I scream, my throat feeling raw as the salty tears burn my eyes. "I loved you. I would have done anything for you!" I grit the words through my clenched teeth and try to grip the chair as I stand on shaky legs.

"I loved you so much. And this is how you treated our marriage. With lies and secrets and all this shit I don't even know about."

"I'm sorry I kept that from you, but that was it." He says "that was it" as if it's easily accepted. As if he's never told a lie or done anything else that would ruin us.

"Liar! How much shit have you gotten into at work?" I let

the words tumble from my mouth, all the rage coursing through my blood. "But you kept at it. You were never going to stop until something made you. You didn't give a shit about me or what it did to us!"

"What kind of marriage is that!" As the words tear from my throat and Evan stares back at me a guilty man, the reality hits me like a bullet to the chest.

I was blinded by my lust for him. Maybe even my love. Either way, I've been blind to the reality.

But I want more. And I deserve better.

"I love you," he says like that's the answer to all of this. Like it will save us.

"You keep saying that, but I don't think you know what it means." *Or maybe love just simply isn't enough anymore.*

"What really gets me," I take in a long, ragged breath, finally taking a step toward him but immediately stop when he does the same.

Standing across from him in the small office I look him in the eyes and get what I've been thinking about out of me. "You saw her all the time. You were with her at every function." My voice lowers as I add, "Even *I* was with her all the damn time. And you didn't bother to tell me."

"What happened was a mistake for her too."

"Don't talk to me like she wasn't some home wrecking whore. She was married! And she knew we were together. How could you? How could you stand to be around her!"

"I was working. If you'll recall, you were broke and we needed money. What was I supposed to do? Quit?"

"Does your boss know?" His expression turns to stone, although he looks more pissed off than anything else. "Does James know?" I ask him again.

"I don't know."

It's silent as I breathe out a huff of disgust.

"I'm sorry. I fucked up years ago."

"It wasn't just years ago. Every damn day you went back was a mistake. Every day you kept it from me was a mistake!"

"What part of it being my job don't you get?" he asks me in a low voice full of anger as he takes another step forward.

"You could have gotten another job." All I can see is red. The words come out automatically, but my mind is racing. My breathing is heavy.

"Who was going to hire me?" he asks me, his shoulders

rising faster as his breathing gets heavier. "You were just starting out and needed every penny I could earn."

"Don't act like you did this for me!" I spit at him with anger. My hand beats on my chest. "Don't you dare blame this on me!"

Tears prick my eyes as he stares at me without saying a word.

Shame and guilt heat my body. Both of us are raging with emotion. Both of us want to tear the other person apart. That realization is all I can take. Tears spill over and I have to turn away from him. With my back to him, he tries to touch me for the first time today and I rip my arm away from him. I shake my head and firm my resolve.

"Please leave me alone. I'm begging you, Evan. If you love me, please get away from me."

CHAPTER 20

Evan

There's no hope in the darkness,
No light to move toward.
There's no way to ease the pain,
No forgiveness she can afford.
The truth I cannot change,
I'm a sinner and I confess.
But I refuse to let her go,
She's my love and nothing less.

I love you, Kat, and I'm sorry.

I text her again, the cellphone screen lighting up the dark bedroom in Pops' house, my old bedroom. The stupid posters reflect the light that scatters into the room in stripes from the blinds on the window. The sound of the traffic is louder here and everything about it reminds me of the life I used to lead. The one before Kat. The one I'm so damn ashamed of now.

I'll never forget the look of disappointment on his face when I showed up a few hours ago with a duffle bag. It's like even he lost hope in me making it right with Kat.

It's crushing to leave her. But it's different this time. It's hopeless.

I feel so worthless and it's never been more apparent to me that my life is meaningless without Kat in it.

I swallow thickly as I lean back on the bed and fall into the flat pillow and close my eyes. I've never felt so alone. I wish I could take it all back.

How fucking childish. I know it is. But in this moment I make a silent wish that I could just go back five years and do it all the right way this time.

As I close my eyes and feel my heart slow and my blood turn cold, I remember one of the last conversations I had with my mother.

She'd seen me with Kat while we were out one night. Just a coincidence, but she kept acting like it was more than it was.

Kat was a fling and a good time. She's someone I wanted

more and more of and I made damn sure to monopolize her time until I had my fill, but of course that time would never come. I just didn't know it back then. Or I liked to pretend I didn't anyway.

"She seems sweet," my mother told me when I came home for Sunday dinner. Looking back at that night now, I realize how much slower she was to set the table. How everything was a little off, but to me, it was just an obligation I had to my mother before I would be leaving to go out and have a good time.

"You didn't even meet her," I laughed at my mom. Shaking my head and taking a drink from whatever was in my cup. I leaned back and looked at my father, waiting for him to agree with me.

"Plus she's the only girl you've seen me with."

"That's true," Ma replied and shrugged. "I like the way you two look together," she added and then looked me in the eyes as she smiled. "Is it too much to ask that you pretend to value your mother's opinion?"

I let out a small laugh and shook my head. "I'm glad you approve," I told her. More so just to make her happy than anything else, but it only opened the door for Ma to invite her over for the next family dinner. I had already started coming up with reasons to end it that night.

It was too much. I was young and in my prime and working a job that would keep my appetite well fed.

I was ready to end it too the next night. But, my God, her smile and the way she laughed at me when I pulled up wearing an old rugby shirt. She thought it was the oddest thing and I'll never forget the way her soft voice hummed with laughter and it carried into the night. Who was I to take that away? I knew she'd end it with me anyway. I didn't know it would be after marriage and five years later.

If I could go back to that night, I would change it all.

"I'm heading to bed." My father's voice catches me off guard and my body jolts from the memory. I pretend to rub the sleep from my burning eyes and clear my throat to tell my father good night. It's tight with emotion and it takes me a second to sit up in bed.

"You look like hell," Pops says.

My head nods and I take a moment to set my feet on the floor. My head is still hung low and my shoulders are sagging as I rest my elbows on my knees.

"How did you keep mom out of it? All the stupid shit you did?" I ask him. I know he led a wild life. He's got the stories and the scars to prove it.

I lift my head and look him in the eyes, forcing a small smile to my face. "I need to know what to do. I need advice."

"You can't. It's gotta stop." He shrugs his shoulders, the faint light from the hallway casting a long shadow of him into the room, ending at my feet. "That's the advice I can give you. Don't keep a damn thing from her. You should already know that."

I swallow, or try to, as a ball of spikes grows in my throat. "What if you can't stop? What if I can't quit this job and this life?" The image of Tony dead on the floor stays firm in my sight. Even as I blink it away and look up at my father, I can still see him. Overdosed and staring back at me as if it was my fault.

I brought him to that room. The one reserved for partying in our company.

I gave him the coke. And then I left him there to get whiskey and cigarettes.

I brought him to his death.

I can never tell her that. I can barely admit it to myself.

"Did you ever mess up so bad, you thought you could never make it right?" I ask, even though his answer doesn't matter. I guess I just don't want to feel so alone.

"We all do; you just find a way. I'm sorry, but it's the best I've got."

"Find a way …" I say the words softly, barely moving my lips as I look at the edge of the comforter, wishing it were that easy.

"I don't know what to tell you, Evan. I did everything for your mom, and I'd do it all again. Maybe that's where you went wrong?"

"What's that?" I'm quick to ask him, my gaze focused on him and whatever it is he has to say. I'm desperate for an answer to all this shit. I need to take it all back.

"You weren't thinking about her."

His words sink in slow, but deep.

I shake my head and agree, "No, I wasn't."

"The best thing you ever did was marry that girl." I nod my head, feeling a jagged pain move through my body. "Worse thing she ever did was let you leave her side."

He doesn't know how true his words are.

CHAPTER 21

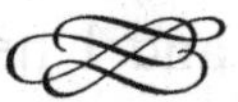

Kat

You left a space beside me,
You left me all alone.
You left a space beside me,
I thought my heart would turn to stone.
You left a space beside me,
Desire creeps in the night.
You left a space beside me,
Lust fills the emptiness just right.

The moon looks gorgeous. The colors of autumn are setting on the city skyline and the beautiful hues of orange and soft reds travel up to the bright full moon.

It's early for it to be out, but as I walk away from the

townhouse, down the stone steps as the heavy walnut door shuts behind me, I can't help but stare at it. There's beauty in nature and having the small bit of it above the city is something I've taken for granted for so long.

With each step my boots click on the concrete, until my body stumbles forward and I nearly fall down the last two stairs.

"Shit!" I cry out as I frantically reach for the iron rail and just barely get a grip tight enough to keep me upright. My purse is flung down to the crook of my arm, spilling gum and my phone onto the busy street.

I mutter beneath my breath as my cheeks heat with embarrassment and I keep my head down. Most people walk around me, and I'm fine with that. Better than fine. I'm happy that they're just ignoring me and my stupid fall.

I crouch down low to grab the fallen items, ignoring them as they do with me, but as I stand up I realize someone didn't miss my fall and their eyes haven't left me.

"You okay?" Jacob says as he comes toward me, nearly out of breath. His cheeks are a brighter red than they were before, the chill of the air getting to him. His hand is cold on my shoulder as he helps me stand upright. His thick, black wool jacket brushes against mine and the heavy scent of pine, a masculine fragrance I love, fills my lungs.

"I saw you from across the street," he tells me as I blink away my surprise. Not only from his presence, but from my reaction.

I brush the hair from my face and give him a grateful smile as the thin crowd continues to walk around us. As I clear my throat, Jacob walks backward with me to stand on the stairs.

"I'm so clumsy," I breathe out and reluctantly laugh at myself as I steady the bag back onto my shoulder.

Jacob shrugs and slips his hands into his pockets as he says, "I expected worse." As he speaks, his perfect teeth show, and I can't help but eye his lush lips. "Honestly, that was a nice save."

A warmth flows through me, but the breeze makes it feel hotter than it should.

"Well thanks," I say, shifting my weight and shaking my head. "What are you doing here?"

"I'm checking out a townhouse down here. Moving to the city was definitely the right move for me."

"And have you thought of the contract at all?" I ask him

and then bite the inside of my cheek. "I don't mean to be forward. I'm just excited to work together," I add.

I don't miss how his eyes stray slightly to my breasts when I breathe in deep. He looks away, toward the street to try to play it off and licks his lower lip. Maybe it was a subconscious thing on my part. I almost feel the need to apologize.

"I'm thinking I should get to signing it. I just was hoping maybe we could meet up to go over a few minor details?" he asks me as he turns his attention back to me.

I smile and nod my head, my hair falling back in front of my shoulders. "I'd be happy to," I answer a little too eagerly. His eyes flash with something they shouldn't. But I ignore it.

"Well, I should get going," the words rush out of my mouth.

"Me too," Jacob says and looks back across the street. "My realtor is over there somewhere waiting on the steps to let me in to 'my dream home,'" he says, mimicking what must be his realtor's nasally voice, and then gives me another view of his gorgeous smile.

"Be safe," he says comically and then takes a few steps forward. "I'll text you," he says over his shoulder and I simply nod. Not able to speak, just standing there, gripping on to my purse strap with both hands and wondering why he gets to me so much.

I won't deny that he does.

And that's not the part that bothers me.

It's why. Is it him? The timing?

What is it about Jacob that makes me want him, when I haven't lusted for a man in years? Well, other than my husband.

CHAPTER 22

Evan

What's left behind but ashes,
When you've burned all around?
What's to be done about destruction,
When your hope has been drowned?
The light is getting dimmer,
The end so close it seems.
There's nothing left but silent chaos,
Forgiveness lost in the screams.

"Have you tried roses?"

My gaze moves from the cell phone in my hand to my father. With his arm braced against the wall, he taps his knuckles against the drywall.

"I'm not sure roses are going to help me," I reply and give him a weak smile.

"You'd be surprised. Flowers are a girl's best friend."

A small, but genuine smile graces my lips as I toss the phone onto the end table. "It's diamonds, Pops. The saying is diamonds are a girl's best friend."

"Then get her diamonds then," he says with a shrug, then makes his way to the worn, caramel leather recliner in the corner of the living room. The game's on the TV. I'm not sure who's playing since the volume is so low I can barely hear it.

"She still hasn't messaged you back?" he asks.

"Nothing yet," I say low and then look back at the phone, wishing it would go off.

"You going back home to talk? Or what's the plan?"

"I don't know," I tell him. "I know she wants space; I just don't know if it's what's best."

He nods his head and says, "It's hard to know. Especially when she's not talking to you."

"I wouldn't talk to me neither," I tell him, mostly out of the need to defend her. "I'd kick me out."

"It was a long time ago," my father says, but there's little conviction in his voice.

It's quiet for longer than I'd like. Both of us not knowing where to go in the conversation.

"I remember when you moved in with her," Pops finally says and breaks the silence.

"It feels like forever ago. I hardly even remember what it was like before her."

"Feels like it just happened to me. All the boxes and her wanting to paint first and then wanting everything in a certain order. She sure has a way of going about things."

I lean my head back, staring at the ceiling fan as I say, "Yeah she does," with a hint of a smile on my lips. "She's particular."

"That's a word for it," Pops says back, not missing a beat.

"You love her though."

He nods his head. "I love her for it, too." He clears his throat and says, "I never told you this, but I felt like I'd lost your mother and then lost you."

"Pops, no-" I try to stop that shit, but he's already moved on before I can get a thought out.

"It was a short-lived feeling. Kat came over more than you did after the move, if you remember."

"She's the one who wanted the family dinners. I remember her pushing for that."

"Probably wouldn't have happened if it wasn't for her."

"I think she was just trying to make things right."

"I know she was. She's a lot like your mother in that regard. You did good picking her."

I can't respond to my father. He's never talked to me about Kat really. Now, of all times, is just making the pain that much worse.

"You remember that heavy ass dresser?" Pops asks me and it makes me huff a laugh as I nod. More than anything I'm thankful for the change in topic.

"She had to have it," I say absently. "It was her mother's."

"Oh, I know. I remember her telling me a dozen times."

"She kept talking about the movers." I shake my head. "We didn't need any movers."

"Sure, sure. I remember that squabble."

"Squabble," I repeat and run my hand over my hair. "She knew I could handle it."

Pops laughs at the thought. A deep laugh, and then he leans back in his chair.

"You guys can handle that, you guys can handle anything," Pops says.

"It feels different though, Pops." I swallow and fight back the swell of emotion. "This isn't just a fight."

"How would you know?" he asks me. "You haven't even really had a fight, have you?"

I stare at him blankly, knowing me and Kat haven't ever gone at it before, not really. A little bickering here or there. But this isn't some argument over dishes. This is worse than he can imagine, and I'm ashamed to even speak the truth.

I'm ashamed to tell him how I really feel too. Like it's hopeless.

"Just get her something shiny. Spoil the woman," he says, throwing his hand up.

I let a trace of a smile linger on my lips as I picture handing Kat a bouquet of roses. I'd pick the really dark red ones, but make sure there's some baby's breath in the package too. One of the real big bouquets. The ones that make you lean in and smell them. Too good to resist. That's the kind I'd get her.

I can see her soft smile as she peeks up at me, holding it in both her hands.

A warmth settles through me. I wish it were that easy. I'd buy every flower I could if that were the case.

"Whatever you do," Pops says, distracting me from the vision of Kat forgiving me. "Just don't give up."

CHAPTER 23

Kat

The past holds me captive,
I just want to forget.
But I'll settle and forgive,
I still love you, and yet.
I can't help but to feel torn apart,
When you promise me no more lies.
Make sure you cross your heart,
Make sure you hope to die.

My fingers keep tapping on my phone and my gaze keeps drifting to the door. He's coming. Soon, too.

Evan needs to get his shit and get out. Mistake after mistake after mistake. That's what this relationship has been. There's undeniable love between us. I won't argue with that. But some people aren't meant to be together and at this point in my life, I should be concerned with having children and not the possibility of having to bail my husband out of jail.

There's a bit of anger that's carried me throughout the last two days. It's what I focus on. It's what gives me the strength to tell him I don't want him anymore. To tell him it doesn't matter when he tells me that he loves me.

I know it matters, and I'd be a liar if I didn't admit that I'll always want him. I'll always want to feel loved like I did when we first got together.

But there's only one way for the story of the two of us to end. And that's with him packing his shit and getting out.

As if he heard my thought, the front doorknob jiggles and the sound of keys clinking creeps into the room.

Fate hates me. It must fucking loathe me because the sight of my husband standing in our doorway shatters my heart.

I try to keep my expression cold, but my body goes numb and the same coldness that swept over my body only weeks ago when I felt my marriage falling apart drifts over my skin now. His eyes are nearly bloodshot. He can't even force a look of anything but agony as he turns his gaze from me and walks slowly into the room, closing the door behind him. I can't look him in the eyes. His disheveled hair and all-around rough appearance makes my body itch to touch him. To comfort him. To make the obvious pain go away.

I think that's why I'll never be able to deny that I love him. The image of him in pain destroys me to my core. My soul hurts for his, and I want nothing more than to take his pain away.

I need to love myself more than I could ever love him. And I'm trying to. My God, am I trying to.

"Hi," I'm the first to say a word and break the uneasy tension in the living room.

He nods his head as he tosses his keys down on the coffee table and stands awkwardly in front of me.

"How are you?" he asks me and it feels so odd. Like we're just old friends or acquaintances. I have to swallow the tightness in my throat and ignore the heat flowing through my body, begging me to give in.

"Not the best," I answer him. I try to find that anger, I remember everything as my eyes shift to the entrance to the dining room, but there's not an ounce of anger that will come to my rescue.

"I miss you," he says as the last word spills from my lips. He doesn't try to hide the desperation.

"I miss you too," I admit, letting my words crack and then lick my lips.

"Things have gotten rough, but I never stopped loving you." His words are raw, coming from a damaged man. "You're the only thing that matters."

"What you say is so right, Evan. But it's what you've done that makes it impossible for me to stay with you."

His boots smack on the hardwood floor as he makes his way to me. And I don't move. I don't object. I even lean into him slightly when he sits down next to me. At first he's pointed away, his elbows on his knees but then he looks at me with a hurt in his eyes that makes me inch closer to him, and he does the same.

I may be angry about what he's done. What I've done as well. But no amount of anger can outweigh the pain we both feel in this moment.

The pain from knowing we're damaged beyond repair.

"Will you ever forgive me?" he asks me and then takes a chance, moving his large hand to my thigh and gently rubbing his thumb back and forth.

"I already have," I tell him and feel slightly less strong.

Weak for being okay with what's happened. Or at least for accepting it.

"Do you just not love me anymore then?" he asks me, his eyes piercing into mine and holding me captive.

My lungs stay still and the words hang on the tip of my tongue. They're too afraid to leave me. I'm so weak for him, so bendable and disposable. If I admit such a flaw, he may never give me a fighting chance for something more.

And what's worse, I may be content with that.

"Please just tell me you love me," Evan whispers. "I know I fuck up, more than I should. But please don't stop loving me."

"I've never felt so alone," I tell him and mean every word. It's one thing to be left alone. It's quite another to choose it. And in this moment, I don't want it. I don't want to be alone another day, but I know I have to.

"I don't want to be alone. I don't want to be mad at you," I tell him, wiping from under my eyes and leaning my body into his. He kisses my forehead before enveloping me into his arms. And I let him. My biggest flaw.

"Then don't," he whispers and then pulls away to look down at me, waiting for my eyes to meet his. "Forgive me, please," he says and when I look to him, his dark hazel eyes beg me. His voice is raw and full of nothing but pain and remorse. "For everything. For being so stupid. For putting you through all this shit."

The question is right there, right on the tip of my tongue. I should ask, I should know what he's hiding. But the look in his eyes is so familiar.

"I meant what I said," I tell him. "I need you to leave."

"But you still love me?" he asks me even though it comes out as a statement.

My body heats, my breath stutters and the words get caught in my throat, refusing to come out. I'm on the edge of leaving him, of ruining this man I love so much.

"Yes, I love you so much," I admit and the confession is like a weight off my chest, but one that only leaves a gaping, painful hole in its absence.

"I can fix this," he tells me.

"I need you to leave, Evan," I plead with him weakly.

"Just give me time."

"We're separated, Evan. That's what that means." A small laugh bubbles from my lips but it's sad and pathetic.

"I don't want this. Please, Kat." Evan closes his eyes and

buries his face in the crook of my neck. I've never seen him so weak. So desperate for mercy.

And I've never wanted to forgive so badly in my life. But it's not forgiveness that I need. It's a different life. And I won't get that with him.

"I'm sorry." My lips move but the words aren't audible, and I have to say it again.

His fingers dig into me, holding me closer and tighter, as if the moment he loosens them, I'll leave his grasp forever.

"I'm sorry, but it's what I want," I tell him and I've never heard such a horrible lie in my life. But he nods his head, pulling away slightly although still refusing to let go.

"It's what I deserve," he says beneath his breath. His eyes are glossy and his breathing slower as he looks away from me, still holding on but trying to gather the strength to say something. I don't trust myself to speak. So I just wait, praying for this moment to be over. Praying for something better to come once this has all left me. But how? I have no idea. I've never felt so dead inside.

"One last time. Please, just once more. I love you Kat, I swear I've never loved anyone like I love you. And maybe it's not enough to keep you, but for tonight?"

Again I don't trust myself to speak. I'm not sure what words would pass through my lips. But I know what I want and I lean forward to take it, spearing my fingers through his hair and pressing my lips to his. It's only when I feel the wetness against our lips that I realize I was crying.

I let him hold me, and I try my best to remember every detail.

The way he smells, masculine like fresh pine and dew.

The way his heart beats just a bit faster than mine as I rest my palm against his hard chest.

I try to remember everything. I pray that I will, because even though he said he can make it right, I know he can't. I know that time will aid in the distance growing. I know we're leading two different lives.

I know I need more, and that I deserve someone who won't hide things from me and make me feel like I've lost myself.

So I need to remember this, because I want it to be the last time.

Not for him, not for us, but for me.

CHAPTER 24

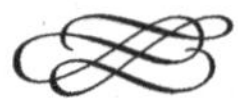

Evan

Don't throw me away, don't tell me you're through.
Don't stop loving me, I can't live without you.
That ring on your finger, that makes you my wife.
You're my everything, my love and my life.

I didn't mean it when I said one last time. I was just desperate for more. All I have to do is be next to her when she needs a single thing. Anything. Just one small crack in her armor. At least that's what I keep hoping for.

It's what's keeping me from dissolving into the nothingness I feel.

I wonder if she'll get over me before that time comes. If

the few years we had together was enough to make her love me even when she doesn't want to. That's all I keep thinking about as I stare at her sleeping form. There's only a sheet over her gorgeous body, hiding it from me. Her back is toward me as she lies on her side, her hair fanned out along the pillow. I've been awake for hours; I'm not even sure I slept at all.

It feels like it's over, but that can't be true. I can't just let her go this easily. But somehow it doesn't feel like letting her go. It feels like I don't have her anymore. Like I don't even have the option to keep her anymore.

A sudden buzz from my phone vibrating on the nightstand strips my thoughts from me and makes Kat stir next to me.

I keep my eyes on her as I reach for it. She slowly turns to look over her shoulder and then looks away, pulling the sheet tighter around her. Closing herself off from me.

My chest feels heavy as I let it sink in that she doesn't belong to me anymore. The bed dips as Kat pulls the sheet with her and walks to the bathroom.

I would think my life couldn't get any lower than this, but the text from James mocks that thought.

There's still so much shit that I need to fix and make

right. So much damage I've caused that's leaving cracks under each and every footstep I take.

Come to the office.

I stare at the text as I hear Kat flick on the light switch in the bathroom, the light filtering from under the closed door. She turns on the water as I put the phone down.

James can go fuck himself.

It's like he knew I'd think that. 'Cause the second the phone drops to the nightstand, it goes off again.

It's not about work. You know what it's about.

I was given new information today.

The texts come one after the other in rapid speed and it makes adrenaline slowly pour into my veins, breathing life into me.

The sound of the bathroom door opening and the light switching off forces me to look up at Kat. She slipped on a robe in the bathroom. It's some sort of black and pink kimono from a bachelorette party I think. I've never seen her wear it but it's been hung up by the towels for years. I guess it's all she could find in there to hide herself from me.

She doesn't return my gaze and I can already see that she regrets last night.

Our last night.

I refuse to let it be true. I refuse to give up. But I'll give her time since that's what she thinks she needs.

"You can come whenever you need to," she says and then pulls a shirt over her head as she lets the robe fall into a puddle around her feet. The sight would make my dick hard as steel if it weren't for the words that hit me at full force. "To get whatever you need or want."

"You really want me to go?" I ask her even though I know I need to leave regardless of what she tells me. I need time to sort my shit out and get my life to be the one that belongs beside hers.

I wish she'd lie to me. I can see it in her eyes, her posture; I can hear it in her voice that she needs me to go. *Tell me a pretty lie, Kat. Make me believe you still want me.*

"I think it's for the best," she says as her eyes flicker from me to the door and she pushes her hair out of her face. She looks so worn out. She's tired of my bullshit.

"I just want to be happy and I feel like we're so used to being something else that it's not going to work."

The argument stirs in my chest, but she's right in a way and I know I can prove to her that we're going to be fine. I just need time. "I'll go now, but I'm coming back when I fix things."

"That's what you do, isn't it? You fix things?" Fixer. That's what they call this job, but really I'm supposed to prevent anything from breaking. There's a small huff of a laugh that leaves her, but it's not the joyous sound I've grown to love so much. And it's because of me. I'm the one that broke our marriage.

"I know we grew apart, but we're still together. Even if you want to pretend like we're not for a little while," I tell her. I take a step to go to her, but she shakes her head slightly, crossing her arms and taking a step back.

"It was only one last time, Evan."

My mouth falls open just slightly for me to tell her last night wasn't the last time. I won't let it be. But the words don't come out. There's no conviction in my thought.

My eyes close as the phone in my hand buzzes again and I don't miss how Kat looks at it, a question in her eyes.

"It's James." I answer her unspoken question

She chews the inside of her cheek and doesn't acknowledge me in the least.

"I quit and I've just got to sign some paperwork." The lie slips out so easily. I'm almost ashamed at how easy it's become to hide the bullshit from her and disguise it as something normal and relatable.

I don't know if she can tell I'm lying, or if she just doesn't care anymore. She leaves me alone with nothing but a small nod in the bedroom we built together.

My blood turns cold and I stare at the open door. The pictures from the hall taunt me. I can hear the laughter. I can remember the softness of her skin when they were taken.

The phone goes off again and it pisses me off.

I grit my teeth as I read the messages.

Get here in the next hour.

Out of spite, there's no fucking way I'll be at his office by then. And I make sure to hit the message so he knows I read it. He can wait.

CHAPTER 25

Kat

Without the truth, there is no trust.
Without the truth, there is no us.
No way to move forward, just stuck in the past.
This marriage is damaged, there's no way it can last.

It's supposed to hurt this much. I keep telling myself that over and over again.

That's what a breakup is. It's pain. It's removing someone you once loved from your life. Erasing them as if they don't exist. As if they've died. And that's the most painful thing one can experience.

That's why it hurts so much. Because I'm supposed to be in agony.

"You look so tired," I hear Jules say before she rests her hand on my shoulder. Standing in my small kitchen, with its clutter and a pile of dirty dishes in the sink, she looks so out of place here. "Are you alright?" she asks me softly.

Before I can answer, the sounds of Maddie and Sue laughing over something drift into the room. The wine has been flowing, and half of the only remaining box of pizza is left on the counter. It's what I said I came in here for, but really I'd just remembered my time with Evan last night and then this morning. And I just wanted to be alone for a minute.

"You can tell me anything, Kat," Jules says in a voice so full of empathy. I've always loved the person she is. But never more than now.

"I don't think I am alright and I don't know if I ever will be," I tell her and then arch my neck to stare at the ceiling, keeping my eyes open and trying not to cry.

"Is it normal to cry so much?" I ask her. "To be this emotional and this exhausted?"

"When you lose someone you love, yes." She says the words so easily, sending a wave of calm through my body, but even that makes me feel that much more exhausted.

"I just wish I was past this stage."

"It'll happen before you know it. One day, the reminders won't hurt so badly. The mention of his name won't cut you to shreds. One day it'll feel like it's supposed to be this way."

"But I don't know if it is," I confess to her and then hear Sue walk in from the dining room.

Her wine glass clinks on the counter as she sets it down. And then she catches a glimpse of me, her expression morphing to one of sympathy. An expression I learned to hate growing up, but right now, while I'm weak and feeling so lost, it's an expression that makes me lean into her when she opens her arms.

"You're alright, babe," she says softly and wraps her arms around me.

"Aw," I hear Maddie coo as she makes her way into the room.

"Let it all out," Sue says but I shake my head, my hair ruffling on her shoulder as I sniffle. Sue smells like wine. She sways a little and squeezes me tight. She's definitely more than tipsy.

"I'm sorry guys. It wasn't supposed to turn into this," I say as I stand up straight and pull my shit together. Sue tries to hold on to me a little longer, but I push her away. I can handle this. At one point in my life I was so good at being alone.

It takes a few deep breaths and Sue filling the empty glasses of wine on the counter for me to get over whatever this breakdown was.

"Don't be sorry. It's a sad time no matter how much you don't want it to be," Maddie's the first to say something and Jules nods. I expect a retort from Sue about celebrating or some shit like that, but she nods as well.

"It's going to be okay though," Jules says and then Sue chimes in with, "You've got us, babe. We'll always be here for you, and that's all you need."

"Well maybe a vibrator too," Sue adds a moment later and a genuine laugh erupts from my lips. It's short and unexpected, and fills the room. But it felt so good to laugh. To smile. To feel anything other than this darkness that's a constant shadow over me.

"Do you want a glass?" Sue asks me, nearly spilling the wine from a glass filled too high as she tries to hand it to me. I haven't had a drink all night.

"If I do, I'm going to pass out." Just as I answer, another yawn hits me. "It's been a while since I've been able to sleep." Well not the nights Evan sleeps with me, but I can't tell them that.

"I'll take it," Maddie offers and immediately sets it back down on the counter.

"So it's really over?" Sue asks and then takes a sip. For the first time, I see something in her eyes I haven't before. Not when it came to me and Evan. I see sorrow. Or maybe I just want to see it.

I nod my head, ignoring how the emotions swell up again. I haven't told them that he cheated on me back when we first started dating. I can't admit it. I don't want to say the words out loud and make them real. I don't want them to see him as a villain. I love him too much to paint him in that light. Or maybe it's the shame that I still love him even after knowing what he did.

"We're just leading two different lives." I shrug and add, "But we always were, you know?"

"And he doesn't want to change?" Maddie asks. There's always hope in Maddie. And I wish I could hold on to that.

"Men don't change," Sue says woefully. "I'm sorry. I'm going it again," she says shaking her head. "Sometimes it still hurts you know? And I don't want you to go through what I did. I promise you, it's the last thing I want for you." Her voice gets a little tight, but she shakes it off quickly.

I love Sue, and I remember how hard her divorce was on her. But I swear this is different. *It has to be.*

"He said he wants to fix it," I answer as I watch Maddie sip from the glass without picking it up. My lips tug into an asymmetrical smile for just a moment at the sight.

"It's not what he says." The hardness in her voice is absent, but there's still a finality in her statement. "Why would he change? He's been this way for years. What would make him want something different?"

It's meant to be a rhetorical question, but the answer rings clear in my head. He did something bad. Something that he needed an alibi for.

I stare at the dark red liquid. Sue's voice turns to white noise as she tells a story about something. I don't know if it's the first time he's needed an alibi. Or the second or the third. But it's the first time he changed. I knew something was off before the article. Before he told me anything. Before the lies.

I knew something was different.

And I didn't even bother to ask him what he'd done.

CHAPTER 26

EVAN

It's not what I did that haunts me,
It's what I didn't know.
Even if it was a mistake,
I know you reap what you sow.
I should have stopped pretending,
I should have moved on long ago.
It's time I tell her everything,
It's time that she should know.

There's a slow prick of irritation crawling down my spine as I sit in the chair across from James. It makes my entire body feel the need to move, like a spider is climbing its way down my back. My fingers dig into the hard wood of the armrests as I stay perfectly still, staring down my former boss. Former friend. Now enemy.

"You aren't the best at listening," he says from across the room as he closes a drawer. The city lights are just creeping in through the window behind him. Casting shadows over the large desk.

"I don't follow orders," I grit between clenched teeth. My words come out menacing, but I don't mean for them to. One more meeting, and this is over. I'm done with him. And he's yet to get the message or to tell me what the hell is going on.

James leans forward, clasping his hands together and his perfectly hemmed suit wrinkles beneath his arms, making the fabric look cheap. He's always looked just a bit cheap. Regardless of the brand or how expensive his tastes are. Some assholes just look like a knockoff.

He taps his fingers on the desk, but my eyes don't leave his. "The reason I called you in here is simple, Evan. The new client we have likes to live on the reckless side, and I'm concerned about drug abuse."

A gruff huff leaves me from deep down in my chest. "I quit." I ignore the fact that he's hinting around what happened with Tony. My skin crawls and that feeling of a spider walking on me comes back. I can't help but think he's recording this conversation. Everything in my gut has been telling me there's a setup.

That I'm going to take the fall for what happened.

But it was my fault, so I should be taking the blame regardless.

"I know what you said, but I assumed you'd come to your senses," he says, waving off my curt response. "Like I said, the new client has been known to behave a bit recklessly and I just want to make sure the policy we had in place remains the same."

The policy. I smirk at him, my grip on the arms getting tighter although my fingers are all that move.

The policy where the clients get what they want, but we don't say it out loud to anyone. The one where we're given clean stashes of the best drugs in the rec rooms. That's the policy. But instead of saying that, I answer, "After what happened with Tony I would think it's more than clear that we should advise our clients against anything too reckless."

James' eyes narrow. He knows I know. That fucker is recording this. I'm not an idiot. The only question I have is why. Why record it? More blackmail? Or evidence? What's he after?

"What is it you really want?" I stare him in the eyes as I ask. "You know you've provided drugs to clients before." I cock my head to the side as I ask, "Are we changing the policy?"

"I've never given anyone anything illegal," he says and I notice how he stiffens slightly but still tries to act casual as he shrugs and adds, "There's no change to the policy."

My wife has this thing she does. It's a smile I hate. A smirk really. I hate it when she gives it to me. It's one that tells me she knows I'm full of shit. And while I sit here, staring at this asshole, I can feel the corner of my lips tug up into that sarcastic smirk. It doesn't stay there for long though.

"Did you know the coke was laced?" James asks me and it takes a moment for the question to register.

The coke I gave Tony.

That doesn't make sense. Our shit is clean and pure and the best there is.

It's also provided to us in the rec room by the company.

"I wouldn't know a thing about that." It's the only answer I can force out. Keeping a hard stare on my face even as my blood heats hotter and hotter.

I know the laws in and out. And I can't admit to any knowledge that could lead back to me. I can accuse him, but not admit to participation or any foresight of drugs being gifted so freely when asked.

I raise my hand as if I'm the one in the wrong. The one

who misspoke. "None of it matters anyway. I told you, I quit."

"And I told you, that you-"

"I'm done," my words come out hard as I stand up and tower over the desk. James is quick to get up, tugging at one sleeve and then the other on his suit. "I thought you had something to tell me. Something useful and not some delusion that you could use to blackmail me."

His eyes glint with a darkness at my words. "It's not blackmail. I haven't-"

"Fuck you, James," I tell him and start walking out of the room. It'll be the last time I come here.

"You know what I can do to you," James says to my back.

"I'm calling your bluff," I say out of anger and instantly regret it, but I don't stop. All the weeks of not knowing if him or Samantha would tell, all the guilt and denial rise up in my chest and the words come out without my consent, "Tell them what happened."

Just the thought of the truth getting out lifts a weight off of me.

"Tell them I gave him the coke. Tell them I set him up to get high and came back to him dead. Tell the press. Tell everyone," I say and my heart beats faster and faster as my hands ball into white-knuckled fists. But then I realize what I've just done. I realize I've said it out loud. But I don't care. It doesn't change anything. None of it matters anymore.

"It's murder, Evan, and you know it," James says as I face the door to leave. Not bothering to acknowledge him in the least.

Yes, it's murder. And it's not the first time something's happened under my watch. But it's the last. I'm done with this shit and this life.

I didn't lace a damn thing. If that stash was messed with, it wasn't me and I'm not going down for a crime I didn't commit. I'll own up to everything else.

I want to pay for my sins and chase what truly matters to me.

A love I took for granted. A love I don't know if I can salvage.

CHAPTER 27

Kat

Pulled in every direction,
Too dizzy to stay still.
My feet stumble beneath me,
My body frozen from the chill.
No more of being numb and weak,
No more of waiting, left in vain.
I've had enough of lies,
I've had enough of pain.

The buzz from the townhouse speaker rouses me from my seat in the dining room. Buzz. Buzz. It's an annoying, high-pitched sound that I can't stand.

My head's already throbbing. It's been like this for hours,

ever since I got home and took the test. I can't go back and look at it. It's hard enough to wrap my head around everything that's happening.

And the guilt ... my eyes close as I walk to the front door where the box is and hear the incessant buzzing again.

As I walk to the front of the townhouse, hustling down the stairs so I don't have to hear that damn noise again, I realize it's nearly nine and I'm still in my pajamas. At least I have pants on, but the matching light gray cotton shirt has a large spot of coffee on the front and I'm sure my hair's a mess.

"Who is it?" I ask in a voice that sounds more together than I feel as I push the button down and then release it. The only person I can think of is Henry, Evan's father.

"Sorry to bother you, I was just hoping for a quick meeting," a voice says on the other side and it takes me a moment to recognize it.

"Jacob?" I ask into the intercom.

"I hope you don't mind, I was in the area and wanted to stop by," he says and his voice breaks up.

I know it's rude to make him wait, it's unkind not to answer him immediately, but this is so unexpected. I don't know how to react or respond.

"I'm not quite dressed for company," I tell him and then close my eyes from embarrassment. He still hasn't signed with the company and I haven't spoken to him since the coffee shop incident.

"That's alright with me," he answers easily and I lean into the button, keeping it held down as my head throbs again and my eyes close with frustration.

"Is it alright if I come up?" he asks, the noise from the box ringing out clear in the small foyer.

"Of course," I answer out of instinct. "Come on up," I tell him and then hit the buzzer to let him up. My heart races as I consider why he's here. I know why, deep down. It's my fault. I led him on.

A sarcastic laugh leaves me as I throw my head back and wipe my tired eyes with my hands. How self-centered and presumptuous I am to think he's here for anything other than business. I ignore the guilt and the worry that riddle my body and glance in the large oval mirror in the foyer as I wait for Jacob to make his way up the stairs.

There are bags under my eyes and a smattering of eyeliner from yesterday still remaining. I wipe carefully under them and pull my hair back, but I still don't look professional. I find it hard to care though as I open the front door.

I'm caught off guard as he walks up the stairs and comes into view. Of course I look like hell when he looks charming in a laidback kind of way. His hair is ruffled, but probably gelled to look like it's slightly messy. It's his stubble though that gets me. I have a type, and Jacob fits that type to a T. Maybe that's how I know this is going to be trouble.

He gives me a wide smile and doesn't seem to care about my appearance in the least.

"I was just going to call it an early night," I lie, trying to stand with dignity in front of Jacob.

"Oh shit, I'm sorry Kat." It's odd hearing him call me Kat. Most of my clients don't use my nickname. It's too casual. A type of casual I usually put an end to immediately. But I can't bring myself to correct him.

"What are you doing here, Jacob?" I ask him warily. We don't have an appointment, and quite frankly I'm not in a state to be professional.

"It's Jake, remember?" he asks playfully and God help me, but I blush. "I was wondering if I could maybe take you out for coffee? I was hoping for dinner. If not tonight, then …"

"I'm sorry, I don't think that's something," I stutter over my words. "Jacob …" I clear my throat and say, "Jake, I hope I didn't give you the wrong impression." I suck in a breath and try to push my hair out of my face.

"It's nothing at all that you did, I just," he takes a deep breath and smiles before letting out a small laugh. "It was stupid of me, I'm sorry Kat. I just thought maybe there was a little attraction on your side?" he asks although it's a statement.

"Jake, I'm ..." I want to say married, taken, in love with another man. The last line would be true. I'll always love Evan, and nothing will ever change that.

"I thought maybe you would like some company," he asks, tilting his head as he leans against the wall. The muscles on his shoulder ripple as he does it. "I went through something a bit ago and I know I could use a distraction."

A distraction would be nice. I can't help that the thought makes me more relaxed each second that passes.

His half smile and gentle sigh are what do me in as he shrugs and slips his hands into his pockets. "I just thought maybe you needed someone. Or you'd like the company." He's handsome when he looks at me like that. It's a look that makes me feel warmth running through me. Compassion and understanding.

I've never been so tempted in my life. I so desperately need someone. The need to fall into his arms and let out every bit of tension and cry is overwhelming. I need the pain to go away; I need someone to take it from me, because I'm a hopeless wreck.

"It's very sweet of you and I won't lie," I start to say and then hesitate to finish the thought, but settle on the basic truth. "I wouldn't act on anything because I just can't right now. I would never forgive myself and it wouldn't be fair to you." My words are rushed at the end, trying to defend my decision and assuage me of the guilt I'm feeling.

"Hey," Jacob says with an easy tone that breaks through the anxiety washing over me. His reassuring voice forces me to look into his gentle gaze. It's comforting and relaxing and makes me not trust myself. "How about this?" he asks as he takes a step closer toward me. "How about you call me if you think you want to hang out or talk, or whatever it is that's on your mind?" he asks in a soothing tone that's almost melodic. It calms me, each word a consoling balm to the hurt that rages through my body.

I want that. More than anything, I want this pain that I feel to stop. I would give anything to make it go away. Jacob could do that, but it would be short-lived. I blink away the haze of lust, the cloud of want and desire leaving me slowly, very slowly. I clear my throat and look him in the eyes as I tell him, "I can't."

"'Cause we're going to work together?" he asks, although the way he tilts his head and strains his words makes it more than obvious that he knows why I can't. My lips form a thin straight line as I shake my head no.

"You love him?" he asks me, and the bit of control I have on my emotions slips.

"I do, but that's not why. I'm just–I'm not okay and I need to figure things out …" I can't finish the thought, but thankfully I don't have to.

"I understand," Jacob says and runs his hand through his thick hair. My eyes are caught in his as I nod in thanks.

"Let's pretend this didn't happen then?" I ask him.

"I'd rather you remember," he says with a grin that makes me crave him more. "I'll be here when you're ready," he says and then turns to leave. To walk away from me and leave me alone in my misery, just as I asked.

For a second I want to reach out and stop him from leaving; I don't want to go back to what's waiting for me. I don't want to face what I have to do.

But my fingers grip onto the edge of the foyer doorway as Jacob turns away and heads to the front door.

"I'll talk to you later then?" he asks as he opens the door to see himself out.

I should say no. I should cut off whatever this is. It's dangerous and I can feel myself slipping toward an edge where I won't be able to balance. I can see myself falling. And that's why I give him a small smile and nod my head.

"Later," the word slips from my lips like a sin.

CHAPTER 28

Evan

I won't stop fighting,
I won't let this tear us apart.
One mistake won't take her from me,
One mistake can't break her heart.
I'll plead with her and do what's right,
And pray that she will see.
She's all I have to live for,
On my knees, I pray she'll forgive me.

The radio in the car is silenced as I turn the ignition off. It's not often I get a parking spot so close to the townhouse. It was a sacrifice we made when we bought the place a few years ago.

My head falls back against the leather headrest and I

stare up at the building, at the top two floors on the the right side, knowing that Kat's in there. So close, but so fucking far away just the same.

My phone pings just as I open the door to get out and drag my sorry ass up to tell her everything. To lay it all out there, beg for her forgiveness, her understanding. But most importantly for her to stay with me.

If she can still love me, after all this shit I put her through and everything ahead of us, then we can get through anything.

But it's not her that texted me. It's Samantha.

I heard you quit.

News travels fast, I respond quickly and then debate on how to tell her I won't be responding anymore to her. That it's not fair to my wife and now that I've left the company, there's no reason to have any type of relationship with her.

What about what happened? she asks and I stare at the text on my phone as the lights in my car dim, signaling me to leave. She follows up the question with another that makes my stomach churn. *He knows about what happened and you know he won't let it go. He'll hang this over your head until he gets what he wants.*

My brow knits as I read the message. I don't give a shit

what he knows or what he wants. For a moment I think maybe she's messaging the wrong person. I settle on my response.

I have nothing to give him.

He knows about us, Evan.

I stare at the text message, letting it sink in.

You told him? I ask her, my gaze shifting from the phone to the lit townhouse building off the busy city street. The lights are on in her office and the living room. So close. She's so close.

My phone vibrates in my hand and I look back down to see her response. *He's known for years.*

My hand balls into a white-knuckled fist as I realize he's been playing me. He's never let on that he knew I fucked his wife.

My first instinct is to blame Sam. *You didn't tell me you told him,* I text and then hate myself for it. I didn't know she was married; we were both high and I wanted any excuse to end things with Kat.

I didn't think he cared.

So now what? I ask her and try to swallow the ball of heat rising in my throat. It doesn't change anything.

I don't see him letting this go. Not when he can get back at you.

A frustrated groan travels up my throat.

Fuck him. He can do what he wants, but I'm not his bitch.

My phone immediately vibrates as I slip it into my pocket, and I immediately take it out. Not to read her response, only to shut it off, silencing it and ignoring all the problems that wait for me.

I swallow thickly and step out into the cool night, the city traffic surrounding me as I shut the car door and leave it all behind.

Everything is crumbling around me, but the only thing I care about is losing Kat. I don't see how I can hold on to her when I don't have a plan and I've lost control.

She needs a better man, and I swear I can be one. We just need to start over and get away from this shit.

I run my hand down my face. Hitting the lock, the car beeps and the bright headlights flash in the dark of the night. The sounds of the city street are loud as I walk up the sidewalk, past men and women who carry on with their busy lives and don't have a clue how mine is being ripped apart.

The keys jingle in my hand as I make my way home. Every second I'm trying to think of the best way to come clean about everything to Kat. She deserves to know, even if she hates me once she finds out. I have to tell her first.

A heavy breath leaves me as I turn the lock and walk into the building, running a hand over my hair and trying to block the image of her disappointment from my mind.

I can see how her green eyes will widen, how her lips will part and how she'll think I'm lying at first. I can see how she'll look at me, how she'll question who I am and why or if, she loves me.

My footsteps are heavy as I grip the iron railing and head to the top of the stairwell, to our home we've built together, the one she's kicked me out of. My gut feels heavy, churning with a sickness that rises to my chest as I hear her voice and recall the memory of her telling me to get out. My fingers wrap tighter around the rail, keeping me upright as I force myself to continue. I need to confess and come clean. But I don't think she'll love me anymore once she learns the whole truth.

That's the part that hurts the most. I barely have a grip on the railing as I take the last step and imagine her telling me to leave again.

When I need her most.

I just want Kat back and the life we once had. It's all I need to live.

My blood turns ice cold when I stop at the top of the stairs and see Kat talking to that asshole from the café.

My legs feel like they're trembling; my body's shaking from the sight of him. Jacob, the supposed client Kat said was no one. *No one, my ass.*

Anger rises quickly as I watch them. I'm not an idiot. I knew there was something between them. I could tell. I know my wife. The thought steals the breath from my lungs and the love I thought I had, the love I thought she had for me, it all crumbles into dust.

"You motherfucker," I sneer the words without thinking twice. The door to my townhouse is still cracked when this prick looks up at me.

"What are you doing!" Kat screams as she stands in the doorway. I turn just slightly, just enough to see her frantically pushing the door open. It bangs hard against the wall as she pleads with me to stop. But there's no way I can.

I won't let anyone come between us. She's all I have left.

CHAPTER 29

Kat

It's not because I hate him,
It's not because of love.
It's because I only have myself,
When push comes to shove.
I knew better than to fall for him,
To think that we had grown.
I knew better than to believe in love,
I'm meant to be alone.

I'd recognize Evan's voice anywhere. But the anger is something new. Something terrifying even. The second I grip the cold handle and open the door, my body freezes and the shock makes my mouth hang open and my eyes go wide. My heart beats in what feels like slow motion.

"Stop it!" I scream at him. My words echo in my head as he slams his fist against Jacob's jaw. It's instantly red and swollen. And Evan's already got his other fist up.

"Evan!" I scream as I run out of the foyer and into the hallway. "Stop it!" I yell and grip onto Evan's arm. I try desperately to pull him away, but his hard, hot body is a force I can't control and I'm still hanging onto him, my nails scratching his arm as I try to pry them apart.

"Evan, stop!" I slam both of my hands into Evan's chest, managing to squeeze between the two men as Jacob grabs his jaw.

"You fucked my wife," Evan yells over me, screaming at Jacob and this time I want to smack Evan straight across his face. I don't. I don't give him any reaction except to turn toward Jacob to apologize.

But Jake is smiling, a cocky grin plastered across his face like this is some sort of joke or game. Like he thinks it's funny, and it does nothing but piss Evan off.

"You mother-"

"Stop it!" I scream again, and this time my voice feels raw and it pains me to scream. My body's hot and shaking, adrenaline coursing through my blood as my heart races.

"Get out of here!" I yell and push Jacob away. His light blue eyes flash with something, perhaps disbelief, or maybe something else. I'm not sure, but I don't have time for him.

"You're cheating on me," Evan says it as if it's a question, his nostrils flaring and his hands still clenched into fists.

"I'm not the one keeping secrets, you fucking asshole. He's a client and nothing more." My gaze almost shifts away from him. I know there was something, a chemistry that kindled between Jacob and me. A tension that I wanted to push. But it's only because I was hurting, and I never submitted to the temptation. I couldn't hurt Evan like that. I never would.

"What is wrong with you?" I ask him with nothing but disdain. For a moment I think of all the questions on the tip of my tongue, asking him why he's doing it and when he turned into this man. But this is the man I married. I'm the one who's changed. Not him.

Evan takes a step forward and his hand raises to my shoulder. I smack him away, barely feeling his hot skin against mine. "Don't touch me!" I yell at him. My hand stings from the impact and I can't stand it.

I can't stand what we've become.

Evan's shoulders rise and fall steadily. The heavy breaths

and furious look in his dark eyes make me take a step back. I'd never think he'd hurt me, never. But the fear spreading through my body forces me backward.

"Kat," he says and his voice cracks, like my name strangles him as he whispers it again. He takes a hesitant step forward, raising his arms and the blood from his torn knuckles is all I can see.

"What were you thinking?" I can barely ask him. Evan's expression falls and he looks past me. It's only then that I turn and see that Jake is gone. "What's wrong with you?"

"What was he doing here?" he asks me and I want to smack him again. How dare he accuse me of anything.

"I've never cheated on you, and I wouldn't. Ever."

"Evan, I can't deal with this. The partying and what you're doing."

"I quit, Kat. I might … I might have some things happen." He closes his eyes and moves his hands to his hair. Hands with split knuckles and traces of blood.

Was he always like this? I want to hold and comfort him. But it's no use.

"I was stupid."

"Evan, you've had years to be stupid. Years of me begging you to grow up." Every word hurts more and more. I know I'm not going to give him what he needs. I can't anymore.

"I wanted you to be my partner." I whisper the words, my voice laced with disappointment.

"I thought that's what we were."

"I need someone who's ready for the next stage of life," I barely get the words out as my throat dries and closes, threatening to suffocate me. But I finish the thought, making my heart split into two as I look deep into Evan's eyes and tell him, "Or no one at all."

"Kat," Evan says, whispering my name as if it's a threat. One against him. Or maybe it's a plea. "I'm sorry, okay?"

My head shakes and the words won't come out.

"I'm sorry I hit him, it looked. It looked like something else to me, but even then I shouldn't have hit him."

"No, you shouldn't have."

"It was shitty of me. I'm sorry. I'm so sorry," he says and I believe him. But it's not enough.

I wipe the tears from my eyes with the back of my hand as I shake my head. "I can't do this anymore." It's the truth and even though it's the worst pain that I've felt in my entire life, I know it needs to be done. "I can do this on my own."

"Don't say that," Evan says, but he stands there numb, not moving, his hands by his side and his body stiff with disbelief. Or maybe fear. "I can't lose you," he says. I feel like my heart is breaking, but I shake my head.

"Maybe I should just be alone." My eyes burn with more tears as I shake my head again and say, "No, I need to. I need to be alone. I'm sorry," my voice fails me as I whisper the apology. I hate hurting him; I can't stand the pain in his eyes and expression. He doesn't try to hide it in the least, and it shreds me.

But we're just not meant for each other, not with the lives we're leading.

"I love you."

"Love isn't enough!" I yell and hate myself. I truly do. "It's not enough anymore," I say, steadying my voice although it's still low. I cross my arms and try to keep myself together, I try to hold my body upright although it begs me to collapse.

"Is that what you want?" he asks.

"I want a divorce," I say the lie as if it were one word. The words all come out at once, bunched together and needing to be said, to be heard. To be felt to the very core of who Evan is.

My fingertips grip onto my forearms as I slowly raise my eyes to his and the conviction wavers.

He doesn't speak, although his lips part once and then again. He licks them as his brow furrows and he visibly swallows and looks past me at the empty wall. Again he starts to say something but stops, clasping and unclasping his hands and trying to find some way to tell me what he's thinking.

The worst part is that I want him to say something. I need him to give me something to hold on to him.

I'd go mad waiting to hear him tell me he'll make this right. For him I'd fall again, I know I would. There isn't enough strength in my body to keep me from Evan.

But he doesn't say a word. It takes a long moment. Each second my heart beats, the steady sound is all I can hear anymore. And then he turns his back to me and walks away without saying another word.

My body is freezing as I slowly turn from the hall and head toward our door. I can't breathe, but somehow I am. I can't manage a thought, but my mind is whirling with the image of what just happened.

The way he spoke my name like he needed me. The way his voice was laced with desperation and his eyes shined with determination, but then failure. The way his expression crumbled when he realized he lost me.

I don't stop walking until I get back to our bedroom, barely glancing at the unmade bed and remembering the last time we shared it and everything about that night. I can still feel his lips on my neck, his hands traveling ever so slowly down my body as he whispered how much he loves me. And I believe the sentiment. No one has ever loved me like Evan, and no one else ever will.

It's just not enough.

For me, I'd go back to him. I'd let him do what he wanted and I'd pay the price.

I pick up the small plastic stick still hanging off the edge of the sink.

My head's been a mess with all the shit Evan's done. I didn't realize I'd missed one period, let alone two.

It's the brightest set of pink lines. I may not be the best friend I can be, or the best wife for that matter. But for my child, I'll be the best mother I can be and that starts with saying no to the life I once lived and had with Evan.

My hand splays on my lower belly as I lean my back against the edge of the sink. I have to tell him and I will, but not yet. I need to stop loving him. I need to move on and focus on what I change and make better for what's to come.

And a life with the two of us, well, now three … that's a life that can't exist.

Not after the damage Evan's caused.

THANK YOU FOR READING DAMAGED. Evan and Kat's story isn't over yet. Scarred is book 2, the final book, in their duet. Have you read the first duet in the Sins and Secrets Series? Jules and Mason's story is not to be missed … have a sneak peek of Imperfect.

Imperfect

FATE BROUGHT US TOGETHER, but the sins of my past threaten to rip us apart.

IN A CITY RULED by corruption and powerful men, only the ruthless survive. And that's just what I am. Like father, like son. The life I lead is riddled with black tie affairs and dark secrets.

A SIMPLE MISTAKE destroyed a woman I knew nothing about. She was only a name and a beautiful face in a photograph. Her fairytale life was shattered, but I didn't give a damn.

OR AT LEAST I thought I didn't care, until she stumbled into me.

One look, and I was tempted.

One taste, and I was hooked.

IT WASN'T SUPPOSED to turn into this. She's a good girl from the Upper East Side, innocent and naive. She's ashamed to be moving on so quickly.

Especially with a man like me. Someone who could tarnish her sterling reputation and make the crack in her picture-perfect frame splinter even deeper.

We both know this was only meant to be a one-time thing. But I'll never have my fill of her.

NOW SHE HAS me wrapped around her little finger, using me to get through her pain. I'm addicted to her soft moans and the way her nails scratch down my back. *I'm starting to need her just as much as she needs me.*

I'll protect her from the truth as long as I can. But even if she finds out, I'm not letting her leave me.

She's *mine* now.

"Love is more than words; my heart can tell you that." - DLS

To Donna, always an inspiration.

PROLOGUE

Mason

Don't let them see.

Her words echo in my head as I stalk toward the quiet bedroom. She whispered them against my lips last night. The cool air slipped between us as she broke our kiss and slowly opened her eyes in the dark of the night.

The street light shined down around us on the back porch of her place on the Upper East Side. The city life slept quietly so late at night, or early in the morning, depending on how you look at it. Only the sinners like us were left awake.

Don't let them see. She left me with the parting plea and here I am… giving into her wish.

I've never crept through anyone's back door so late at night. Not once in my life have I had to sneak around like this.

I don't want to keep doing this shit, but here I am. What the hell has this woman done to me? *I'm wrapped around her little finger.*

It's because she's ashamed. I know that's why she doesn't want people to know we're together. Not just a fling, not a rebound fuck. There's something more to us now, but she doesn't want the world to know.

The floorboards creak under my weight and I hesitate in the doorway, the dim lamp from the hall filling the dark room with a hint of light. It's her place and her neighbors aren't going to hear, but I don't want to disturb her.

It's obvious she's sleeping, but she stirs beneath the silk duvet until finally she opens her eyes and sees me. She tilts her head to the side as she looks at me, burying her cheek into the pillow, a soft smile playing on her lips.

"I missed you," she says and her voice is laced with an equal mix of sleep and lust.

If only she knew the real reason I crave her touch. The reason I'm so tempted to break all my rules.

"I'm sorry I'm late," I tell her in a deep, rough voice as I start unbuttoning my shirt. A smirk turns the corners of my lips up as her eyes sparkle with humor. She doesn't care when I come and go, so long as I lie in her bed at night, or she in mine.

Her doe eyes stare back at me while I slip off the button up and let it pool into a puddle at my feet. I yank my tight white undershirt over my head and look back to see those lush lips parted.

She likes what she sees. My muscles ripple as I let the tank drop to the floor, the moonlight bathing the room and the two of us in a faint glow.

She may want to keep this a secret, but she fucking wants me and she can't hide it. I've become addicted to the way she looks at me like she needs to touch me to stay grounded, just as she needs to breathe air to survive. I've learned to crave the faint sounds of her quickened breath as she waits for me to come to her. *As if she'd die without me.*

I'm slow to unbuckle my belt as my eyes roam down her curves. She's mine to take. Mine to touch. *Mine to keep.*

If it were up to me, I'd take her ass outside and into the middle of the busy city street to show the world that she belongs to me now. I don't want to sneak around anymore and I don't give a shit who knows. I'm tired of this bullshit.

The the anger boils in my blood as I grip my leather belt tighter, making it sing in the air as I pull it through the loops and drop it to the floor with a loud clack. All the while my gaze is on her gorgeous eyes, and she's staring back at me with the same desire as I have for her.

The past is over and done. No one will ever know what really happened -- not her, not anyone.

"Mason," she practically whimpers my name and it pulls the beast in me closer to her. My knee dips into the bed, making it groan with my weight as I crawl over to her.

Her soft blue eyes pierce through me, cutting through the dark room. More of the soft lighting from the city slips into the room as the heat kicks on and the curtains sway. The way the light kisses her skin as she pushes the duvet away makes her all the more more beautiful.

She's laid out for me. *All for me.* She fucking needs me.

I crush my lips to hers and dig my fingers into the flesh of her hips as she spreads her thighs for me. Her soft moans fill the hot air between us.

She's ashamed to be moving on so quickly. Especially with a man like me. I wasn't made for a woman like her. I'm someone who could tarnish her sterling reputation and make the crack in her picture-perfect frame splinter even deeper. To say I'm rough around the edges is putting it lightly, but I have what it takes to keep her.

We both know this was supposed to be a one-time thing. But now, I want more.

She thinks she's ruined, but she's fucking perfect. It's my sins and my secrets that could destroy us both. I'll never let them come to light. Not now that I have something worth fighting for.

She doesn't know it yet, but I won't stop until she's mine.

She needs to get over it and just accept this for what it is.

She's fucking mine now.

CHAPTER 1

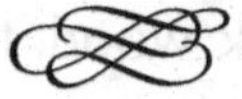

Mason

Sinful pasts will haunt us both.
They never leave, they stay like ghosts.
You can't outrun them.
You can't hide.
When they come back to life,
They'll all know you lied.

"You should be thanking me for covering up your mess," my father says from his high-back desk chair. His fingers grip the leather arms and the tips of his thumbs rub gently back and forth across the brass studs.

Though the blinds are closed, the tall windows behind

my father fill the large office with the dim light from the evening sun.

I look over my shoulder at him, still holding a random law textbook I've taken from the floor-to-ceiling shelves that line the side walls of his office. The room smells of old books. With the dark wood, tan leather and deep red Beaumont rug, the decor reeks of old money and that's exactly what this room represents.

That and bullshit.

Lies and corruption are what have held this room in its current state for generations. I've pretended for so long that it wasn't true. But learning about what my father's done… I can't turn a blind eye to it anymore. It's undeniable and unforgivable.

I huff a small laugh, not letting him see how affected I am. "For the last time," I tell him as I shut the book and smirk at him, "it wasn't my mess."

I'm not admitting to shit. Not even to my own father. In this city, one slip up could send you tumbling into an early grave. Like my mother and like the mess my father's referring to. I don't trust him. I don't trust anyone any longer.

My father's eyes turn to slits as his face reddens before picking up the cup of hot coffee. He holds the black mug with both of his hands, blowing across the top and refusing to acknowledge me.

"You would have gone through hell-"

I cut my father off, although my voice doesn't reflect any emotion whatsoever. It's a turning point in our relationship. Instead of him getting me worked up, it's the opposite. "No I wouldn't have." I look him in the eyes as I add, "I would have been just fine."

A moment passes and the only sound is the ticking of the large clock on the right side of the room. "It wasn't my mess you cleaned up, and we both know it." He's the first to look away, but instead of showing remorse, he only looks pissed.

"Did you need anything else?" I ask him. I just want to get the fuck out of here and back to the construction site. This office reminds me of my grandfather, a man I loved and trusted. But he was a man who turned out to be just like all the rest of the powerful men in this city. Ruled by sin.

"I'm tired of you getting into trouble," he finally says. He's lost his fucking mind. This is the first time in my life I've truly been in control of myself. No more fucking around. The recent events have been sobering. When I was a hormone-filled teen dealing with grief and anger, it was easy to pick fights. First, the death of my grandfather and then my mother. It was easy to act out.

Thirty-three is too fucking old for that bullshit. I finally have my life together… all but the ties to my father. It's a tangled mess of lies and money. Much like everyone else's dealings in this city.

The thought makes my eyes fall to the floor and then look back up to the shelves to mindlessly scan the spines of the ancient texts.

Knowing what my father did makes all those memories of losing my mother surface. My stomach churns and my blood heats as adrenaline courses through me, adrenaline pushing me to confront the man I no longer know.

I clench my hand into a fist and bring it to my mouth as I clear my throat and take a few steps towards him. He's the one who called this meeting, demanded it really. But he hasn't even risen from his chair. Lazy fucker.

"I don't know what you're talking about," I answer him easily. "I haven't got a single problem on my mind." I give him a polite smile and keep the charming look on my face. It only makes him angrier and I fucking love every second of his pissed-off expression. He thought I'd feel as if I owed him.

But I don't owe him shit.

I may be just like him in looks. Tall, dark and handsome, or so they say. A brilliant smile with an air of ease that's made to fool and seduce the best of them. It makes sense that he's a lawyer. Really it's a family business really, but if it wasn't, it'd still be the profession most apt for my father.

"You need to quit this shit and do what you're told, Mason." My father stands from his seat quickly, his chair rolling backward and smacking against the wall. It hits the blinds and streams of light flicker into the room.

"I don't need to do shit." He could talk to me like that all he wanted back when I was a child or before I knew the truth, but now I have no respect for the man in front of me. I'm disgusted by him and caught on the edge of what's right and wrong. I should turn him in and let him rot in jail. I grit my teeth as I stare back at him. It's what's right, but I can't bring myself to send my own father to prison.

A low hum of admonishment deep in his throat makes the smirk on my face widen into a smile.

"I have my own company, my own life-" I start but my father cuts me off. Nothing new there.

"You were born a Thatcher, and you'll die a Thatcher." The words leave a chill across my skin. That's the core of the problem. I was born into this shit and I can't run from it. And my company is in debt to him. It was a rookie mistake I made before I knew what I was doing. Back when I didn't see him for the man he really is.

"Why do you even give a fuck?" I finally ask him. His pristine reputation is just fine now that I'm an adult and I've moved on from the fuck-up I used to be. "I'm not the one coming to you-"

"*She* did," he answers simply, with a spark in his eyes and the corners of his lips upturned as if that's all the ammunition he needs. And in some respects, he's right. They all know where I come from. They know I have money and power behind me. And that's all anyone in this city cares about anyway.

I shrug my shoulders and walk closer to the desk, bracing myself by gripping the back of the chair opposite him. "You decided to deal with her when what she said was a lie." I stare him in the eyes, willing him to tell me again how he *saved* me. It's complete bullshit. "She didn't have shit on me. She couldn't have done anything!" My voice rises and I hate that I've shown him this weak side of me.

Control. I thrive with control.

A heavy breath leaves him as he gazes back with pure hate but he doesn't say a word. I knew he wouldn't. He's wrong. Dead fucking wrong and utterly ruined if I open my mouth to anyone. He did it so I'd owe him, but in reality we both know that he owes me now.

"It's your fuck up, not mine." I practically spit out the words and shove the chair forward as I turn to leave him. My body's tense and the anger is increasing. I try not to let it show. I fucking hate that I can't control myself around this prick. Everyone else I can handle, but my own father, not so much.

"Mason!" he calls after me. His voice turns to white noise as the blood rushing in my ears gets louder and louder, drowning out all the bullshit.

The second I open the office door; he shuts the fuck up. He'll never let anyone hear us fighting. *Never.* Secrets are always left in the office. It's a family rule.

The door shuts with a loud thud and as I walk down the empty hall, the thin carpeting mutes the sound of my black leather oxfords smacking against the ground at an incessant pace.

Miss Geist looks up from her spot at her desk. Her eyes wrinkle as she tilts her head and gives me that smile that she always has for me. It's one that says, oh what have you done now?

Through the years, even after my mother's death, Miss Theresa Geist has given me that look. She's the only one who that showed any genuine regret when I had to deal with my mother's passing.

Weak, pathetic. You never let them see. That's all I got from my father and grandfather. Everyone else is dead and gone.

She clutches the small pendant on her thin silver necklace and her reprimanding smile changes to something more reserved when I look back at her. It's instantaneous and makes me halt in my steps. I know I must look pissed. And I am beyond furious. It's been two days since my father told me what he'd done all those months ago. It makes me fucking sick. Of course I knew what he'd done back then, deep down. I knew, but he never admitted it. He didn't have to though.

"He's being a prick," I mutter beneath my breath, waiting for the old lady to be a little bit more at ease. She doesn't know a damn thing that goes on behind these walls, and I don't owe her an explanation, but I can't help myself.

"Now, now," she says with a bit of playfulness although she's still shaken. She's not used to seeing me like this.

I give her a soft smile and wink, putting on the act I use so well. Maybe I have a soft spot for her, but I know who she works for and money is everything in this city.

"Have a good night, Mr. Thatcher," she tells me as she

shuffles the papers on the desk, seeming somewhat less disturbed.

It's enough that it settles me and I push the double doors open with both hands and keep moving. The sound of my shoes slapping on the granite and the open air of the lobby filled with chatter soothes me.

But only for a moment.

It's not until I leave the building that my true feelings surface. The mask fades, and the fear sets in. I didn't know what my father was capable of.

I had an inkling, but I thought I'd always imagined it. I'd thought my memories weren't quite right. It's not that I expected more from him. I just fucking hate that I was right.

What's done is done and I can't stop what's been set in motion.

CHAPTER 2

Julia

Don't leave me alone, I cried and I screamed.
Don't leave me alone, my whole life demeaned.
You left me unguarded. My heart raw and bleeding.
You left me forever. The pain there left seething.
You left me here weak. Just a stone in the ground.
You left a place beside me, my pathetic life unbound.

Blood red lips. It's called Black Honey, my favorite color. I've worn it since my freshman year of college and although I've dabbled in other colors at times, it's always been a staple in my beauty bag. I rub my lips together and smack them once as I look at myself in the mirror.

My skin's looking flawless with the Dior Airflash makeup

and just a hint of blush I'm wearing. My lashes are thick and long. It's a timeless look, classic and clean. And it hides everything. My reddened skin and the dark circles under my eyes are nowhere to be found.

I don't look like the person I've become. This woman in the reflection, she's who I used to be. A very large part of me wants *this* woman back. I want to smile like I used to and hear the sound of a genuine laugh from my own lips.

My heart pangs at the thought though.

He'll never laugh again. It's as if any small moment of time that passes where he's forgotten for even a second is a disgrace. My eyes fall and I slip the cap back onto the tube of lipstick, tossing it into the pouch on my vanity.

No matter what I do, every little thing reminds me of *him*.

Trivial things, like the color of the granite he insisted we purchase for the remodel. The knobs on the bathroom drawers he hated and never failed to mention. Or the change he left in the cup holder in the Bentley. The small pile of dimes and pennies that clink together when I drive over speed bumps or a pothole. The same coins I refuse to touch. He put them there, and I can't bring myself to move them.

So stupid. Fucking pieces of copper renders me useless.

It may seem pathetic, but not to me. From my perspective, I'm being as strong as I can. I face the New York City judgement every day, putting my smile on and taking care of my life the best I'm able.

All the while I shove everything I'm feeling deep down inside. That's healthy, right?

I won't let them see me crumble. They want to. Oh, do they want me to. I can practically hear them licking their lips.

It was all over the papers when it happened.

Julia Summers, born into wealth and raised on the Upper East Side. She always did everything by the book and married young to her high school sweetheart, Jace Anderson. With a loving family, a handsome and doting husband and the social life every young woman in Manhattan dreams of, Jules had a perfect life. Until her husband suddenly passed away at the young age of twenty-eight, leaving the twenty-seven-year-old woman widowed and alone for the first time in her life.

Twenty-eight now.

They're waiting to see what I'll do next. Pens to the papers and cameras ready. There's nothing better for the gossipmongers.

They'd love to see me fall and I have, but not in front of

their eyes. I'll keep my hair pinned up and my makeup flawless.

I know what they say though. They don't need to see the truth to figure it out themselves. There are whispers of alcohol. I don't have enough money for discretion; all my employees have sold out to the papers for a hint of what goes on behind these walls. When you live on the Upper East Side, every single person who struts in front of my home is looking for a crack in my veneer.

What's ironic is that there's no glamour here. Nothing noteworthy in the least. Just a woman who cries herself to sleep still. A woman who's struggling to move on. I suppose it's what I get though. I loved the cameras and lived for that spot in the gossip sections. This is what I deserve.

Days turn to weeks and weeks to months. Now that my husband's been gone for nearly eight months, I have plenty of cracks in this so-called perfect life. I'm fucking shattered.

I look back at myself and think, *I won't let them know it,* as I tug my dress down just slightly and smooth out the black lace.

I clear my throat as I turn off the light, snatching my phone and checking the text again.

Are you sure you don't need me to pick you up?

Kat's a sweetheart. She's always looking out for me. Of all my friends, she's the one who still texts me religiously, which is insane because she's constantly working and I have no idea how she finds the time.

My fingers *tap tap tap* away an answer. *No thank you. Leaving now.*

The Penrose is only twenty minutes away if there's no traffic. Seeing how it's 9 p.m. on a Friday night, I'm prepared to sit in the back of the taxi for half the night.

A light sigh slips past my lips as I bend down to pick up my Louis Vuitton heels. They have a row of spikes up the back and a hot pink underside. They have exactly the touch of color and attitude I would've worn back then. I almost second guess the simple black dress I've picked out. It's a nod to Audrey Hepburn. But looking over my shoulder in the darkened bathroom mirror, all I see is an option for the funeral.

But I would've worn this back then. Back when I was happy and everything was how it was supposed to be. And don't I want to be that girl again?

I grit my teeth, holding the heels in one hand and the iron banister in the other as I descend the winding staircase.

I'm not *that* woman any longer, I've changed. I accept that, but I don't fucking like who I am now. Eight months of a pity party and being stuck in a rut is quite long enough, thank you. I'd like to say that Jace wouldn't want to see me like this… but I don't even know what Jace would want for me. I've quit wearing my ring, although it still sits on his nightstand. I'm ready to move on. I'm ready to find out who I really am.

Before I open the door, I glimpse out the large stained glass window in the foyer. It's all grey outside, and the hustle and bustle below is only a fraction of what it could be.

A faint patter of rain greets me when I step outside. I don't bother with an umbrella, simply tossing a trench coat on and quickly taking the steps to the street out front and hailing a cab. My heels click as I quickly wrap the belt tightly around me and tie my coat.

I could have called for someone to do this, to order me a cab so it would be waiting. I could ask for help with so many things. I'd rather do it myself though.

The breeze and rain feel *real*. The rain is cold to the touch and I'm sure I'll be regretting it soon. But it's something different. And I don't want anyone's help. I just need time.

A cab pulls up within seconds and I lower my arm.

Climbing in and shaking off the gathered rain from my jacket, the inside of the cab is warm and welcoming. I push the hair out of my face and say, "Penrose, please."

"You got it," the cabbie says as he looks over his shoulder to look at me. His thinning black hair is oiled over and he's more than a little overweight. The buttons on his striped shirt are straining to keep it shut.

I can see the questions in his eyes, but just as he opens his mouth to ask *something*, I don't give a fuck what, I turn to look out of the closed window.

Everything outside is wet and dreary. The people walk quickly and a couple only about ten feet away are fighting over an umbrella. It's a cute little fight though and the tall man in a navy blue Henley lets the woman win. She's dressed for business, while he's in casual attire. But as soon as she takes full control of the umbrella, she walks closer to him and he wraps his arm around her waist.

I rip my eyes away and pick at my nails. It's little things like that I find unbearable. I bite the inside of my cheek and hold down the bitterness.

Luckily, the driver gets the picture. I'm not in the mood to talk, and the cab moves ahead, taking me away from my sanctuary and toward another test.

That's what these things really are. Tests.

It's only in this moment that I realize I'm really doing it. I've put it off so many times. I've given so many damn excuses for not meeting up with the girls.

Why today? I don't know. My heart sinks thinking that maybe I'm really getting over his death.

As much as I want to be the woman I used to be, happy and carefree, I don't want to forget him.

I lay my head back on the headrest and close my eyes, my Jimmy Choo clutch in my lap. Jace gave it to me last Christmas. I snort at the thought, running my fingers over the smooth hot pink leather. Really, I picked it out and he paid for it.

I close my eyes and take in a deep breath. It's calming, so damn calming driving in a quiet cab at night in the city. The quiet rumble of the engine and the white noise of the rain are a serene mix.

The last day I saw my husband was when we were watching my nephew Everett, so my sister could have a mother-daughter day with Lexi.

The thought of my nephew brings a smile to my face. With sandy blond hair that just barely covers his big blue eyes and a wide smile, you can't help but smile back at him. He was only a few months old back then. A brand new life in this world. That's the way it works, isn't it? Life and death going hand in hand.

I look forward, my eyes popping open and I stare out of the windshield when we stop far away from Second Avenue where the bar is located; it's just a bit of traffic is holding us up.

The cabbie shrugs as he says, "We should be out of it soon." He's tense at the wheel, probably expecting me to snap at him, maybe blame him for taking the wrong route. More guilt washes down on me. I hate spreading negativity. I don't want other people to see me and judge me, or feel as though *this* is their fault. I'm not an ice bitch… or at least I don't mean to be.

I give him a soft smile, pulling my dress down slightly and placing my clutch in the middle seat, "I figured we'd run into something," I say easily. My voice comes out even and calm. It's the voice I use with my family. The kind of tone that says, *I'm okay, just tired.*

The cabbie shifts, making the leather seat grumble and he tries to make small chat.

I nod my head and answer politely, but keep everything short and to the point. I can be accommodating to others and I want to be. I'm tired of being alone and pushing others away. It's just harder than I thought it would be.

After a moment of quiet, I look out of the window again. The rain's nearly stopped, and instantly the sidewalks are crowded as a result. The people were always there, just waiting under the awnings for protection. Not many people like to venture into the harsher nights with weather that washes away your makeup, and ruins even the best put-together look.

But they were waiting and ready to keep moving just the same. All they needed was a small break before they'd set out again. The only question is if there will be an awning to save them when the brutal downpour comes back.

The cabbie stops and my eyes whip up to the sign on my right, my heart beating faster as I watch dozens of people walking in front of me on the sidewalk. Each going wherever it is that life has taken them. I don't know if I'm ready, but I'm here. My time is up and they're tired of waiting.

"Miss?" the cabbie asks. I shake my head slightly with quick motions and play off my hesitation, paying him and leaving a big tip as well. He deserves it for having to suffer my company.

"Have a good night," I tell him as I slip out, my heels hitting the slick asphalt and the door shutting behind me with a deafening click.

CHAPTER 3

Mason

The wind is harsh and brutal,
It makes you want to run.
The rain will cleanse your poor soul,
As it makes you come undone.
You can seek shelter from the damage
But its refuge is not your friend.
You knew from the beginning.
You knew how this would end.

It figures it would stop fucking raining the second I get in here. The bar is jam-packed as it always is, and the sounds of people chatting and glasses clinking welcome me. I can get lost in the crowds of people. I know they see me, but they don't *know* me.

This bar in particular is one of my favorites. It's always full. It's tufted leather seats are constantly filled, and the warm rich tones of the wooden ceiling and brick walls make it feel like home somehow.

My suit looks like every other fucker's suit. Well most of them. I run my fingers through my hair and shake off the rain as I shrug off my Armani jacket and toss it over the bar top at the very end.

It's been a long fucking day, and the last thing I need is go home alone. As soon as I lift my eyes lift, the bartender on me. Patricia's her name I think. She's in here every weekend.

"Whiskey?" she asks me. She never stops moving, shoveling ice into short glasses and pouring liquor like a pro. Unlike the other women in here, she's not looking for a man with deep pockets. She doesn't do chitchat either, which is one reason why I like sitting in this section. The other reason is that it's out of the way where I can just blend in and watch.

"Double," I answer her with a nod and slip out my cell phone out from my jacket pocket. I've only been gone for two hours, but I've got a dozen emails waiting for my attention. A huff of a grunt leaves me as another text from Liam pops up.

You coming out tonight?

Already out, I answer him as the glass hits the polished bar top and Patricia slides it over to me.

My phone pings as I lift the glass to my lips and let the cool liquor burn all the way down and warm my chest.

Where at?

I contemplate telling him. I like Liam. A lot. If I had any friends, he'd be one of them. But I don't trust anyone and after talking to my father today, I don't want to be around a damn soul.

A sarcastic laugh makes me grin as I realize I've come to a crowded bar to be alone. It's the truth though. In this city, you're always surrounded; there's never a place to hide unless it's in plain sight.

I down the rest of the liquor and tap the heavy glass against the bar top as I consider what to tell him. And that's when I hear it. Almost as if daring me to stay alone any longer. It's the gentle sound of a feminine laugh. It's genuine and it rings clear in the bar even though it's soft.

It's a soothing sound, a calming force in the chaos that surrounds us. As if everything is moving around me but the woman who uttered that sweet sound.

The smooth glass stays still as I look down the bar in search of her.

The rest of the crowd doesn't seem to notice, they continue with whatever the fuck they're saying and doing, but my eyes are drawn to my left. Through the throng of people, I just barely get a glimpse of her.

Blonde hair that's pulled back, showing off her pale skin covered in black lace.

A man at the very end leans away from the bar, digging into his back pocket for his wallet and giving me a clear view of her.

Those lips attract my gaze first. She licks her bottom lip before picking up a large glass of deep red wine. The color, from this distance at least, matches her lips perfectly. She smiles at something someone must have said and her shoulders shake, making the dark liquid swirl in her glass and bringing a blush to her high cheek bones.

She tosses her hair to the side, it's damp from the rain and her fingers tease the ends as she brings her tendrils over her shoulder, wrapping them around her finger while she sips her wine.

It's when she looks away from whoever she's been giving her attention to that my heart stops and my curiosity is piqued.

Without their eyes on her, her expression morphs into

something else. I finally see her eyes, the lightest of blues with flecks of silver speckled throughout, and that's when I really see her. Not just the image of what she's portraying.

Pain is clear as day.

It's the lie though, how fucking good she was at hiding it, that's what really gets me. Even I was fooled.

People can hide behind a smile or a laugh, every fucker in here can pretend to be something and someone they're not.

The truth is always there though and I'm damn good at recognizing it. Your eyes can never hide two things: age and emotion. Hers speak to me in a way nothing else can.

But had I never looked just then when she thought no one was watching, she never would have shown me willingly.

She straightens her shoulders and I see her profile, her expression and the corners of my lips turn down. Not only do I know her pain; I know her name. I know everything about her.

Julia Summers.

My blood chills as she turns back to the table and the smile slips back into place on her face just as the man at the end of the bar takes a step forward, obscuring her from my vision. As if the moment of clarity and recognition was just for me in that moment. Like fate wanted me to know how close I was to her.

I keep my eyes on the bar, doing my best to listen, but her voice is silent or lost in the mix of chatter throughout the crowded place.

“Another?” Patricia’s voice sounds close, closer than she usually is. I lift my head to see her standing right in front of me, both hands on the bar and waiting.

I nod my head with my brows pinched, shaking off the mix of emotions. This city is a small place with worlds always colliding, but I’ve never seen her in person. Only in a photograph. Only that once. I’m sure it’s her though. I’ve never been this sure of anything.

The ice clinks in the glass and I watch as the liquid slips over each cube, cracking them and filling the crevices.

“You okay?” Patricia asks me. It’s odd. In the year or so since I’ve been coming here, she’s never bothered to make small talk. It’s why I don’t mind her.

I give her a tight smile as I reply, “I’m fine.” I reach her eyes and widen my smile, relaxing my posture and leaning back slightly.

She eyes me warily as she mutters, “You don’t look fine.”

It takes me a moment before I shrug it off and say, "I'm alright, just tired."

She nods once and goes back to minding her own business, sliding me the whiskey and moving back to the other customers.

I tap my pointer finger against the glass, looking casually down the bar.

She's hidden from view, but I know she's there.

THE FIRST DUET in the Sins and Secrets Series, starting with Imperfect, is available now. I hope you love reading it as much as I loved writing it.

BEST WISHES,

Willow xx

ABOUT WILLOW

More by Willow Winters
www.willowwinterswrites.com/books/

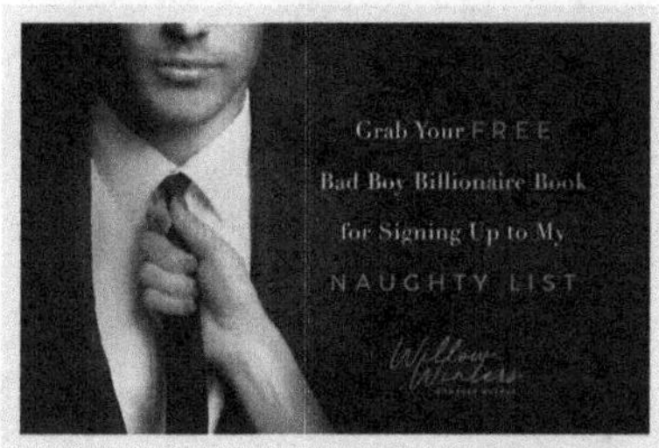

Sign up for my Naughty List to get all the newest romance releases, sales, great giveaways and a FREE Romance, Scandal → Go to my website to join!

Stalk me everywhere!

WillowWintersWrites.com
WillowWintersBadBoys@gmail.com

JOIN MY NAUGHTY LIST

SOCIAL LINKS:

Follow me on Bookbub
Follow me on Twitter
Like my Facebook Page

Check out my Begging for Bad Boys Facebook group for ARC invitations, Freebies and New Releases from your favorite Bad Boy Romance authors.

Happy reading and best wishes,

Willow xx

Printed in the United States
by Baker & Taylor Publisher Services

Printed in the United States
by Baker & Taylor Publisher Services